THE NEW WORLD PROJECT

BY:
CHARLES LUNA

CHAPTER I

Date – October 20th, 2014. The United States has spent the past three years mired in a deep recession. Unemployment rates are at a fifty year high. Home values finally hit rock bottom after twenty consecutive months of decline. Severe storms have battered the country's coastlines, as erratic weather patterns wreak havoc across the world. Instability reigns in North Korea, Iran and Russia as rogue regimes remain in power. Political campaigns are in full swing as the 2016 presidential election is a year away. The country is divided as political parties clash while trying to find a way out of the economic disaster that has plagued the country. The federal deficit is spiraling out of control after several failed attempts to reverse the fiscal downfall. Soup kitchens are overflowing and homeless shelters have waiting lists. Crime rates are escalating as the world's largest economy is teetering on the edge of disaster.

Location – Georgia Tech University men's dormitory.

Late every Saturday night, Wes Holland had an alarm clock that always went off, the other students on his floor getting home from a long night of partying. Wes was always perturbed when this happened because he could not get back to sleep. Partying was a way of life for most college students but Wes was enrolled at Georgia Tech to change the world, not kill as many brain cells as possible before his Monday morning engineering classes. Saturday night October 20th started like every other Saturday night since school had resumed. Unfortunately for Wes, it would not end that way.

"Not again" Wes said out loud as he tried to cover his ears with the down pillow that had been his sleeping companion since the age of two. The idiots were back and were screaming at the top of their lungs.

"Rains is going to puke" one drunk screamed.

"Let's record it and put it on U-Tube. Go get your video camera" another inebriated partygoer answered.

Wes slowly lifted his head and glanced over to the other side of the room to see if his roommate had returned, but he found an empty bed. There were several drunks camped in the hall outside of his room so he knew that rolling over and returning to his dream was not an option. He glanced at the blue digital numbers on his clock and thanked God that he could sleep in on Sunday. The big gulp Mountain Dew that he had consumed after dinner had completely made its way through his system so he flipped on the lamp by his bed, threw on some shorts and a t-shirt and made his way to the communal restroom.

"Go to bed you idiots" he blurted to the partiers as he wiped the sleep out of his eyes on his way to take a leak. Wes was a really laid back guy except when his sleep was interrupted for no good reason.

"Sorry to wake you sleeping beauty" one kid sarcastically replied as he slowly sipped on what was surely his last beer of the night.

"Lighten up dude" another chimed in. "It's college, live a little."

Wes did not reply because he didn't have the energy or the patience to argue with his drunken hall mates. He was an old man living in a young man's body. He did not understand why people would voluntarily drink themselves into a state where they could not control their actions.

The shouting began when he was in mid-stream with his eyes closed and his head resting on the wall above the urinal. At first, he wrote off the commotion as just another idiot trying to be funny, but he knew something wasn't quite right when he heard "Down on the ground, NOW!"

The disturbance was occurring down the hall near where the students had been sitting on the floor near Wes's room. He strained to finish his business then made his way to the door of the bathroom. He slowly and quietly opened it just enough to peek his head out to see what was going on. His eyes bulged out of his head as he watched four men dressed in all black military garb in the hallway. One had an assault rifle pointed at the three students in the hall. They had their noses to the ground and their hands were above their heads as sobriety re-entered their brains immediately. Wes continued to scan the hallway as the adrenaline rushing to his thumping chest and the sick feeling in the pit of his stomach fully awakened him.

The other three warriors had machine guns ready to fire and were preparing to make a forced entry into Wes's room! He lived six doors down from the bathroom and he counted the number of doors just to make sure that it was his room. Panic set in as he was unsure of what to do or where to go. He was barefooted, in shorts and a t-shirt on a cold night and to top it off, he was on the third floor.

"Where is he?" one of the masked men asked the three petrified drunks.

"Where is who?" one answered in a whiney voice that clearly stated he wanted his mommy.

"We want Wes Holland" the masked man answered.

"Who are you and what do you want with Wes?" asked the leader of the drunken students.

He immediately regretted the question as the assassin pointing the gun at him leaned over and squeezed a pressure point on his shoulder. The young man was in so much pain that he couldn't make a sound. He tapped his hand on the floor to show defeat, silently pleading with the killer to release his grip.

"He just went to the bathroom" the poor kid screamed after taking a second to recover from the torture that he had just endured. "It's down that way" he pointed while keeping his nose to the ground.

The four trained soldiers immediately sprinted down the hall to catch their prey. The bathroom door sprung open with one swift kick and the crew stormed the room with special forces type precision.

"Clear" shouted one warrior as he flung open a stall door to reveal an empty toilet.

"Clear" shouted another as he checked the second stall but came up empty.

"Clear" shouted a third warrior as he exited the vacant shower.

"Suspect is on the run. Repeat, suspect is on the run" said the leader of the four man death crew into a small headset attached to his ear. He rushed to the open third floor window and peered into the dark grounds below in search of his target, finding nothing.

After taking a moment to recover from the three story leap that he was sure had broken one of his legs, Wes ran as fast as he could through the dormitory courtyard leaving a trail of trampled oak leaves behind him. He then sprinted across Techwood Drive and scaled the fence to Georgia Tech's football field, Bobby Dodd stadium. He continued to run through the tunnel that led from the outer walkway into the stadium itself. The stadium was darkened as a half moon allowed for a bit of illumination on the field where over forty thousand fans had cheered the Yellowjackets onto victory just twelve hours before. Wes took a seat to lick his wounds and try to make some sense out of what was going on. His labored breath produced small clouds in front of his face as he closed his eyes to relax and think.

His bare feet were stinging as he had not run barefoot outside since the age of eight. His body was aching from taking the brunt of a three story drop into a group of bushes that had somewhat cushioned the blow of his fall. His left knee was writhing in pain and blood trickled down both legs from the sharp branches of the bush that most likely had saved his life. He was out of breath, out of shape and seemingly out of time. He knew why the soldiers were after him but he had no earthly idea who they were, who had sent them after him and if the orders were to kill him or take him alive. He needed a plan and he needed it quick. The soldiers were no doubt professionals, campus police did not carry around machine guns. He was outmatched and knew that he had to leave immediately. He would look suspicious to anyone that saw him because he was half naked on a cold night in October. There was one matter of business that had to be attended to before he could leave the campus. It was what the killers were after and he wouldn't leave without it.

The panicked college student quickly made his way around the stadium from an interior walkway to the north end where he exited the stadium, scaled the fence and darted across the street between two frat houses as quickly as he could so as not to be seen. Luckily, he found a party that was in the last stages of life. He entered through the front door of the all brick three story mini mansion and fortunately went unnoticed as the few remaining partygoers were heavily buzzing and deep into an argument about the day's football game as Bob Marley played in the background. He silently made his way through a fog of smoke, up a flight of stairs and luckily found an empty bedroom. Wes had never stolen anything in his life but desperate times called for desperate measures. After two minutes of frantically searching, he wore a pair of jeans, a long sleeved button up shirt, new socks and shoes and he also took a cell phone. He found a Georgia Tech baseball cap that would be pulled down low on his head and a jacket to fend off the frigid temperatures. He exited through the back door without even raising a hint of suspicion.

It was only a matter of time before the strike team would find him so he could not spare a second. He sprinted around the side of the frat house before ducking behind a car as a black Suburban slowly made its way down Fowler Street, no doubt searching for one very important college student. His eyes watered from a combination of fear and sweat as he prayed that he had not been spotted. He sat in silence, not even daring to take a breath and waited for the vehicle to pass before making his way very quietly to his next destination.

Russ Chandler Stadium was about one fourth of a mile from the fraternity house. Wes carefully but quickly dashed through back yards of fraternity houses until he finally saw the darkened light towers of his favorite venue on campus, the Georgia Tech baseball field. The great stadium backed up to the football practice field and it was there where his secret was stored. He made his way over a fence and walked along a large brown brick wall that separated the baseball field from the rest of the campus. Wes had spent many afternoons watching his favorite baseball team in action and he never dreamed that he would be on the run and having to dig up the information that was his life's work. It was hidden directly underneath the scoreboard, a secret location that no one would ever find. After digging six inches into the softened earth with his fingernails, he hit metal and knew that his secret was safe. He pulled the tiny box from the hole, opened it and removed the disk that had caused his turmoil.

With the disk secured, Wes knew that he had to get off campus or he was a dead man. He hated to get her involved, but his new girlfriend was the only person on campus that he knew with a car so he reluctantly dialed her number with his stolen cell phone.

"Hello" a sleepy but sensual voice answered.

"Megan, I am so sorry to call you this late but I need your help."

"Wes, what's wrong?"

"I am in some trouble and I will explain it later but I need you to pick me up right now. Leave very quietly and I will be waiting for you on Sixth Street behind the baseball stadium."

"Wes, you are scaring me. Tell me what is going on?"

"Megan, do you trust me?"

"Yes, you know that I trust you."

"Then hurry up. I just really need your help right now."

"I'll be there in a minute."

Minutes seemed like hours as Wes made his way through a door in the big brown wall and hid behind a huge old oak tree waiting for his girlfriend to arrive. Every sound startled him and every shadow was a killer waiting to shoot him. The air was frigid but fresh. He had only been dating Megan for a month and a half and he dreaded bringing her into this mess. He had been reluctant to date her in the first place, but her beauty was unavoidable. He was relieved to see the headlights of her Honda Accord slowly creeping its way towards him.

"Make a right and let's get off campus now!" he demanded as he jumped into the slowly moving vehicle without even a hello.

Megan Alexander obeyed her boyfriend's command but had no idea why he continually looked behind them to see if they were being followed.

"Wes, I deserve an explanation. You call me in the middle of the night, ask me to pick you up and then tell me that we need to leave campus. If you want me to help you, it's time to start talking."

"Megan, I swear to you that I will explain everything but right now we have got to get out of here. My life is in danger."

They drove off of the Georgia Tech campus, into Mid Town Atlanta and onto I-75, which was the quickest way out of the city. Every building that they passed gave Wes relief as he was one step closer to escape.

"Where are we going?" she asked after five awkward minutes of silence.

"O.K., I can breathe now" Wes replied as he closed his eyes in an attempt to calm his frazzled nerves. "Here's the deal. I have created a research project for my mechanical engineering class that will change the way that we live. I'm talking about everyone on the planet. Not only is the plan workable, but it is so good that apparently the word has leaked out to some very important people."

"So what's the big deal? Why are people trying to kill you?"

"I'm still trying to figure that out Megan. It could be any number of groups that are after me. The plan was created to improve the quality of life for everyone but it would basically end several major industries as they operate today."

"That is a vague answer to a very important question. I want to know what I'm stepping into."

"You aren't stepping into anything except taking me to where I need to go. Look, I am not going to tell you anything else because I don't want to put you in any kind of danger. I couldn't live with myself if something happened to you." Wes used the sleeve of his jacket to wipe the sweat off of his forehead. He hated being vague to his girlfriend but he knew that it was in her best interest.

"Well that is just great. My boyfriend has got people chasing him and wanting to kill him and he won't even tell me why. Who are you anyway? I thought that I had met a normal guy but apparently you aren't normal at all. I don't want this drama and I don't need this drama in my life right now."

"Megan, I don't want to fight with you. That is the last thing that either of us needs right now. You just have to trust me. I am going to figure this out. I just need some time and I need for you to be patient. I am a normal guy but my research project is anything but normal. Please just drive."

Wes stared at his girlfriend as the lights of Atlanta disappeared behind them. Her full head of auburn hair was pulled back into a ponytail. Her flawless face looked amazing and beautiful without a stitch of make-up on it. Her full lips were trembling and he wanted to kiss them. He wiped away the lone tear that was easing its way down her cheek from her mesmerizing blue eyes as he rubbed her shoulders while she drove them down the interstate. His focus was solely on his beautiful girlfriend which is exactly why he didn't notice the flashing blue lights approach behind them.

CHAPTER 2

"Oh crap! What do I do, what do I do?" Megan pleaded as panic overcame her.

"We're in an Accord, we can't out run them so just pull over and play it cool. We are just out for a drive."

"What do I say? Wes, this is bad."

"Don't say anything. Just answer his questions. But keep crying."

Megan pulled over to the side of the interstate as Wes closed his eyes hoping that a miracle would occur.

"Hello officer" she started as she rolled down the window. The officer was in his mid forties and stocky with a perfectly manicured goatee. He was not smiling as one hand rested on his holstered gun.

"Miss, do you know why I am pulling you over?"

"No sir, I do not. What is the problem?"

The officer suspiciously looked into the front seat of the car. Wes stared straight ahead, trying his best to remain calm. The officer whipped out his flashlight and peered into the back seat then moved the light straight into Wes's eyes.

"Has anyone been drinking tonight?" the officer asked with a grim voice.

"No sir" Megan answered.

"Who is your passenger?" the officer asked.

"My boyfriend" Megan answered in the most calm voice that she could muster.

"I need driver's licenses and an ID from each of you."

"Oh God" Wes thought to himself. Whoever was after him had obviously gotten the state police involved. This was it for him. He was finished. His pulse quickened as his heart beat out of his chest.

"Sir, I didn't bring any identification with me" Wes said.

"Here is my license and registration" Megan added while trying to steer the attention away from her boyfriend.

"If you haven't been drinking, then what are you two doing out at 3:00 in the morning? And miss, I can see that you are upset. Tell me what is going on here." The officer had released the grip on his gun and crossed his arms while demanding a response.

Megan spoke up "Well sir, we had an argument tonight. It is our first fight and we decided to go for a drive to try to work some things out."

"Has he hurt you?" the officer asked just looking for a reason to pounce on Wes.

"Gosh no, it's nothing like that. We are just trying to figure some things out."

"Well, your right tail light is out so you need to get it fixed Monday morning."

"Yes sir, I will."

"And you two need to get home. It is too late to be out."

"Yes sir, we will head straight home" she answered.

They both breathed a sigh of relief as the officer made his way back to his cruiser. What could have been disastrous turned out to be nothing at all. Megan pulled back out onto the interstate and resumed driving while obeying the speed limit and every other traffic rule that she could think of.

"O.K., where am I taking you?" Megan demanded.

"I've got to lay low for a few days to figure out my next move. I can't be seen in public. I used to visit my uncle in Cumming every summer. There is a Microtel there. Take me there but let's swing by Walmart on the way so that I can stock up on groceries. It is open all night and I need some other necessities. I will ditch this cell phone and buy a pay as you go phone at Walmart and we can talk that way. I know its crazy, but I have to think this through."

"Wes, don't take this the wrong way, but I don't know what to think of all this. We have only been dating for six weeks and now this. It is more than I am looking for right now and more than I can handle."

"I completely understand. All that I ask is that you don't tell the authorities where I am. Will you at least do that for me?"

"Yes. And I am not breaking up with you, but I need some time too. I need to digest this whole thing. Wes, you can't use your credit card because they will trace it and know where you are."

"I've got it covered. I buried a couple thousand dollars with a disk that I retrieved just in case anything happened."

"You mean that you planned for this?"

"Not really. Not for something like this."

They made their way to the Walmart in Cumming, Georgia which was a forty mile drive from the Georgia Tech campus. Wes tossed the stolen cell phone into the Chattahoochee River on the way. The Walmart was busier than they expected at 4:00 A.M. on a Saturday night. The freaks were out as they entered the building.

"I want to get in and out of here and get you back to your dorm safe and sound" Wes commented.

"That is fine with me" Megan replied. "I am exhausted."

The 4:00 A.M. greeter was not as happy as the regular greeters. Instead of a smiling face, Wes and Megan received a grumpy nod upon their arrival. Walmart was the same at any time of day. It was a one stop shop for many Americans. You could get your eyes fixed, have a family photo taken, fill your prescriptions, fill your cupboards and buy just about anything else that you needed to run the household. Pallets filled the aisles as the third shift workers were stocking the shelves for the morning rush. Wes and Megan walked down the aisle straight in front of the entrance out of habit. It was genius on the part of the Walmart executives as they wanted shoppers to pass by the jewelry and electronics departments before attending to the pressing needs that caused them to go there in the first place.

"What the….." Wes said as they passed the LCD televisions. "Megan, we have a problem."

Megan was eyeing the winter jackets in the woman's wear aisle as she turned to see what Wes was talking about.

"Holy crap. Turn it up."

They made their way to the empty electronics department and could not believe their eyes as their Georgia Tech student identification pictures were on display on every television in the department. They inched closer to the display and Wes raised the volume button on one of the many televisions.

"This is an alert to all residents in and around Atlanta. Federal, state and local officials are searching for two fugitives. They are both students at Georgia Tech and are wanted in connection with the murder of Georgia Tech professor Harold Michaels. Professor Michaels was found dead in his home this evening, the victim of an apparent gun shot wound to the head. There was no sign of forced entry so it is believed that he invited the killers into his home. The two students, Wes Holland and Megan Alexander are considered armed and dangerous. Should you spot the suspects, please contact authorities immediately. A man hunt is underway and it is believed that the two suspects are traveling on I-75. A state trooper pulled the couple over early this morning on a routine traffic stop as they were headed north bound on I-75. The suspects are driving a nineties model Honda Accord with the license number 875VGW. We will report any additional information to you as it becomes available."

"No! No! No! This is horrible" Wes said in an understatement.

"We have got to get out of here" Megan replied.

"Let's get what we came for, go through the self checkout and leave without looking suspicious."

Luckily the Microtel night manager was not watching television. She was just very perturbed that someone wanted to rent a room just before the sun came up. She did accept cash with no identification and Wes rented the room for a week by paying cash in advance. The hotel was accustomed to visitors paying by the week as families worked through issues, businessmen looked for a cheap rate and people that were recently evicted from their homes looked for a roof to put over their head. They unloaded the food and clothes that were purchased in cash at Walmart then Wes drove the vehicle to a vacant lot, removed the license plate then jogged the two mile route back to where they were staying. Megan was weeping on the bed when he returned.

"Who is Professor Michaels?" she asked between sobs.

"He was my mentor and we were working on the plan together. He was like a second father to me and just in case you are wondering, no I didn't murder him."

"I wasn't wondering Wes. I know that you wouldn't hurt a fly."

"I can't believe that Professor Michaels is dead. In a lot of ways, he has given me direction in life. He was a world renowned researcher, he had a brilliant mind and he taught for the right reasons. He was never a by the book kind of guy. He asked the probing questions that made you really think and use every ounce of intellect that you possessed. I just can't believe that he is gone." Wes buried his head in his hands as he mourned the loss of his hero.

"Who would want to kill him?" Megan asked.

"Whoever killed him is the same group that wants to kill me. We were in on this project together. It was my idea but he was right there with me throughout the process to help turn a concept into a realistic working model. So in a way, I am responsible for his death. I just didn't pull the trigger. I never thought it would come to this."

"Well honey, you and I are in it together now, so you might as well tell me about this plan of yours that has put our lives in danger. I mean where can I go now? I'm wanted for murder right alongside you. My mug shot was right next to yours. Our lives are ruined, and it's all because of a stupid school project. If you care about me at all, tell me now!"

Wes settled into the couch that faced the bed in the small carpet stained suite. A mini kitchen was off to the left with a make shift table next to the kitchen. He knew that he needed to come clean. His dream of two years had quickly turned into a nightmare. The plan was going to be his and Professor Michael's crowning achievement. It was a plan so extreme yet so simply concocted that it was achievable.

Wes adjusted his rear to sit up for the presentation. His plan had recently ruined his life but it was something that he was still very proud of.

"Well Megan, we are in this together now whether we like it or not. I am going to share this with you, but you have to realize that once you know this information, there is no turning back."

"There is already no turning back Wes Holland so get on with it."

"The concept is actually pretty simple. Have you ever watched a screen saver with objects jetting all over the place but never running into each other?"

"Yeah, I guess."

"Computers tell those objects what to do. They can guide those objects anywhere that they like. The computer is the brain of the screen saver. It is programmed to control the screen."

"That is not brain surgery Wes."

"I know that smartass. Keep listening. I developed a transportation method that would completely change the way that people and goods are moved around the country. Instead of vehicles being driven by humans, computers would transport people and goods around the country by using electricity. A six inch metallic strip would be inserted down the middle of every lane of every road in the country. This strip would even go into your driveway. There would be no more cars, no more trains and no more trucks. Trams would be used instead. Did you ever go to Disney World as a kid?" he asked as Megan listened intently.

"Yes, we went three times."

"Well then think of the monorail. Your tram would be on a six inch track and underneath the ground, your tram would connect to an electrical charge that powered it. You would pay as you go with a meter that runs like the meter on your house does. These trams would be powered very inexpensively and would get you to your destination very quickly. They would use sensors like the sensors that are being used by foreign car companies now to prevent you from hitting a pedestrian or animal and since the tracks are run by computers, there would never be crashes."

"Wes, this is way out there."

"By the end of this conversation…"

The phone rang as the two jumped in unison. Megan sprang from the bed to answer the call.

"Listen, I don't know what you two have done, but the cops are on the way. You have about two minutes to get out of here."

"Let's go NOW!" Megan screamed.

"What is it?"

"The front desk said that the cops are coming."

Wes grabbed his money, cell phone and a bag of food and followed Megan out of the hotel room in a full sprint. They could see the blue lights and hear sirens blaring as they rounded the side of the building and made their way in the early morning darkness to the Accord. A team of police cars surrounded the Microtel less than a minute after the escape. Still other cars were scanning the area, in search of the wanted fugitives. After sprinting for a mile and a half, they ducked behind a dumpster at an abandoned gas station to catch their breath.

"We can't go back to the Accord" Wes said. "It's too risky and cops are going to be combing every road in this town. I spent five summer breaks here and I know where we can hide but it's going to be about a five mile hike. Can you make it?"

"We don't have a choice. Let's just get out of here."

Wes was tired of being on the run and he knew that he wasn't very good at it. The police were always going to be one step ahead of him. He had traveled forty miles away from the scene of the crime and was found within two hours. If they stayed in Georgia, they were sitting ducks. He needed time to figure out a way to prove himself to the officials and he was certain that if he was caught, whoever was after him would make sure that his story was never told.

The trip started with a sprint across Georgia 400, a major highway that went from Atlanta up into the North Georgia Mountains. They then started the process of ducking and darting behind dozens of commercial establishments, moving quickly but carefully while avoiding all major roads. They crept through the empty Forsyth County Fairgrounds then sprinted across the County Courthouse lawn. After walking through the playground of Cumming Elementary, they jogged the last mile to their final destination, his uncle's house. He knew that he would be safe there for at least a few hours because his uncle spent every winter in South Florida and they hadn't spoken in years. His uncle had never married but the house where he resided was owned by his long time live in girlfriend. The key was still hidden where it had been six years ago, so the two exhausted fugitives finally had a place to rest their weary bones.

"You catch some sleep for a few hours while I watch the windows and then we will trade" Wes said.

CHAPTER 3

Megan was too exhausted to argue so she curled up in the guest bedroom and passed out from exhaustion. Wes planted himself beside the front window but out of view and forced his eyes open. He tried to digest Professor Michael's murder and the ridiculous accusation that he had pulled the trigger. It was a set-up of grand proportions and if he wanted to live, he had to find out who was behind it all. College was supposed to be a period of time when kids discover who they are and what they wanted to be. Wes knew what he wanted to do before he ever stepped foot on campus. He just needed some direction to make it happen. He chose Georgia Tech because of Professor Michaels. He knew who he was long before attending college and he didn't need to sew any wild oats. He simply wanted to turn his dream into a reality.

Wes was dozing in and out of sleep when Megan walked into the living room to relieve her boyfriend.

"I still don't understand" she started.

"Don't understand what?"

"Why this is so important. O.K., so you have a way to move people around the country by trains. And it will save money and gas. Do you really think that everyone in the country would agree to it? This isn't worth dying over."

"Oh, but it is. Let me finish the story that I started and maybe you will understand everything better. First, everyone will not move around the country in trains. I call them trams. Initially, we will simply retro-fit our cars of today to run on the metallic track. It will be a simple conversion and will cost about $500 per vehicle. So every family will have a vehicle just like they do today, but instead of running on gas, the vehicle will run on electricity. And instead of driving, we will enter our destination into the computer. We then just sit back and let the tram do its thing."

"There is no way that you can convert a car for $500 to do what you say it is going to do."

"Yes we can. And we will. Here is what you need to understand. The computer that we will use in the cars is not that sophisticated. The computers that run the system are very high tech. Think of it this way. Your cell phone does amazing things now, would you agree?"

"Yes"

"Your cell phone is fairly inexpensive and does some cool things. The phone itself is not that sophisticated or expensive to purchase but the system that allows it to do those cool things is very sophisticated. The metallic strip that will be retrofitted onto every vehicle is not that sophisticated but the system that it links to will be very high tech."

"I guess I can see where you are going."

"We will be able to move around the country at speeds that are unheard of, up to five hundred miles per hour on the interstate. There will be no traffic lights because computers will run the entire system. Imagine getting to where you need to go without lights. There will be no fatalities from car crashes. Thousands and thousands of lives will be saved every year. And we will be able to do it relatively cheaply. A family can travel for half of the cost of a gasoline engine. And that is including a federal tax on every mile that will pay for the infrastructure of the system. When the infrastructure is paid for, the federal money will pay for programs to improve the country and pay off the federal debt. It also includes a state tax that will pay for schools and upkeep of the track."

Wes was getting excited as he continued. "Imagine traveling to the Grand Canyon and it only taking you a few hours to get there. Think about traveling to the gulf coast to spend the afternoon at the beach and it only taking an hour. You could live in Atlanta and work in Birmingham and get there faster than if you were making a thirty mile commute in rush hour today. People will be able to travel around our country and see things that they would never see. Tourism will go through the roof and families will be able to visit these places cheaply because the cost to get there is half of what it cost us now. And it will be a pay as you go system, just like gasoline."

"How in the world do you plan to generate enough electricity to power this system?"

"That is the great part about the entire plan. Gasoline will be a thing of the past. I think that everyone now agrees that global warming is real. Our weather patterns are way out of whack. Storms are stronger, droughts are longer and ice-caps are melting. That is a fact. Everyone's focus has been on reducing emissions from vehicles. This system will eliminate emissions entirely. We are talking about a plan that will completely change the course of the dangerous path that we have been heading down for decades. The system will be powered by a combination of wind, solar, hydroelectric and nuclear energy. We developed the system so that these combinations work in tandem and there will never be an interruption of power. There are backups for the backups. The computer system that runs the operation has so many moving parts working in tandem that it will never be interrupted."

"O.K. fine, it is a great plan. Then who is after us?"

"I have no idea. It could be the federal government. We have a president that is in bed with oil companies. It could be the oil companies themselves. It could be an oil rich regime that doesn't want to see this come to fruition. It could be an airline company or even a shipping company. I just don't know."

"How do they even know about it? If this plan is top secret then who leaked it?"

"Professor Michaels knew everyone. He kept a low profile but his rolodex had so many important people in it, you would be floored. And we had gotten to the point where the system was developed and it was time to implement it. He had contacted the president and several members of his cabinet to brief them on the basics. He also had friends in the upper levels of the auto industry. You have to remember that Georgia Tech is on the cutting edge of research for a lot of industries. Some of the greatest inventions that have changed the world were developed at universities."

"I'm scared Wes. If the people that are after us have connections all the way up to the White House, then we don't have a chance. What are we going to do?"

"I'm working on it. Don't give up yet. The thing that we have on our side is that our country needs this. It will be the largest redistribution of wealth that we have had in this country in decades. And it will not be some kind of welfare program for the poor. Every family in this country will be saving money. Real money. If you cut the cost of travel in half for every family in America, then every family is going to have more expendable income. Once the retrofitted vehicles are flushed out of the system, the cost of a family tram is going to be minimal compared to the vehicles that people are buying today that have engines and costly required maintenance. And the system will generate profit for states and the federal government on the taxes that are collected. Income taxes will go down and we will still pay for federal programs and reduce the national debt. This is an open minded politician's greatest dream. And the program will create tens of thousands of jobs when the track is being built. Tourism will boom, restaurants will boom and entertainment will boom. This is exactly what our country needs to get out of the economic slump that we are in."

"Yeah but what about all of the jobs that are lost?" Megan asked while playing devil's advocate.

"It's a slippery slope. And I haven't even told you about the second part of the plan yet. Companies like UPS, Fed Ex and the US Postal service will still have a place in the new world, but they are going to have to reinvent themselves. If an individual needs to send something to Texas, they could get it there in a couple of hours but it would cost the same as driving there. So shipping companies will still operate by sending large amounts of goods around the country but consumers will demand that it be done overnight and in the same day in some cases. Drivers for shipping companies will be a thing of the past. Domestic airline travel will be over. Oil companies will be out of business and our reliance on foreign oil will be finished. Thank God for that. Pizza delivery will be at your home in fifteen minutes and there will not be a driver to tip, a shipping box will just show up. Every restaurant and every grocery store will ship goods to their customers and have them there quickly. Their business will boom but we must retrain the people that will be losing their jobs to perform the new jobs that will be created. Logistics will become an important department in every restaurant, grocery store and retailer."

"So it gives online shopping an entirely new meaning then."

"Absolutely. If my favorite restaurant is one hundred miles away, I can place my order and have warm food show up in an hour. If you wear a hole in your jeans, you can have a new pair to you before you need to go out that night. The way that the world operates is going to change and the companies that change with the system will reap the rewards. Auto makers will become tram makers. Instead of focusing on miles per gallon, they will focus on amenities. And the great thing is that no one has to drive. You just punch in the address that you are going to and sit back and enjoy the ride. Trams will have televisions, couches, microwaves and refrigerators. And it will be interesting to see which automakers survive. The cost of trams will be as low as one thousand dollars for a basic get you to your destination vehicle. And I'm sure that luxury trams will pop up and be the status symbol that cars are today. Alcohol sales will boom because there will be no designated drivers, everyone can indulge and not worry about it. Couples will want to go out and party more because they can party together. Sophisticated campgrounds will pop up because families will purchase RV like trams with beds to save on hotel rooms. Hotels will have to be on top of their game to offer luxuries to entice travelers to get out of their trams."

"I'm starting to get it now. You are talking about changing the world. Everything that we do will change."

"And it is a change for the better. No more reliance on foreign oil. Think about it. Why should the greatest country in the world allow Middle Eastern dictatorships to set the price of our fuel? Stock prices rise and fall over the cost of a barrel of oil and all that we have done is sit back and take it. For years our political leaders have talked about alternative energy like it is some Wizard of Oz pie in the sky idea that is somewhere out there. No one has figured it out. We can check e-mails from our cell phones, we can converse with someone across the world with the touch of a button, we can send someone to the moon, but we can't move ourselves across the country without using gasoline. It is crazy."

"You're right Wes but change scares people. Especially a change this big."

"It only scares people if your leaders are scared and don't want things to change. I don't think many people were scared when Henry Ford built the model T. It was cool. We have lost our ambition in a lot of ways. Change is good, especially when it is going to improve life for most people, it is going to get us out of debt and clean up the place where we live. Why do you think so many people have asthma now? Because our air sucks. We don't even know the damage that we are doing to ourselves. And now we can clean up the environment and improve our means of transportation. It's a no brainer."

"It's not a no brainer either. If it was, then we wouldn't be on the most wanted list right now."

"The people that are after us are complete morons, if for no other reason than our world dominance. We owe China a ton of money. Think about it. Our status as a super power is up in the air right now. We are in debt up to our ears. Our military is stretched thin. Our financial system is in trouble. We have got to re-establish ourselves as the dominant force in the world and this system is going to do it. The New World is going to be introduced by the United States. We will sell this technology to every country and maintain our status as the elite power in the world. Our national deficit will be a surplus and all will be well."

"You are delusional. My God Wes, listen to yourself. We're wanted for murder. Your plan is awesome, I swear to you I think that. But no one is going to listen to you. The man that you worked with to put this plan together is dead and everyone thinks that we killed him. Someone very important doesn't want this New World of yours to happen. If you think it is going to happen, then you are stupid. Figure out how to get us out of this alive. The plan is over, it's done. You need to deal with it."

Wes was fuming at Megan's assault. He needed to get some fresh air so he put on his baseball cap and went for a walk around the block. He needed time to think. Maybe the plan was just a pipe dream. Maybe it wasn't worth dying for. He certainly had not planned to drag Megan into his predicament. She didn't deserve it and he felt terrible about it. If they turned themselves in, he knew they had no chance. They had to keep running, at least until he thought of a better plan. He didn't have an alibi for the murder of Professor Michaels. He had been asleep since 11:00 that night by himself in his dorm room. He thought about having Megan turn herself in and claim her innocence but that was too risky. He needed to find out who was after them.

Wes's daydream was ruined with the sound of a police helicopter circling near the neighborhood. The search was on and he knew it. The walk around the block quickly became a jog back to the house.

CHAPTER 4

"Pack your stuff, we're out of here. We can take my uncle's old truck and drive through the Appalachian Mountains."

"Where are we going?" Megan asked.

"Have you ever been to Kentucky?"

"Not for any length of time."

"Well, my brother doesn't know it yet, but he is going to help us out of this mess."

With a full tank of gas, they headed through the Appalachian Mountains, a slow winding drive but it was an escape route nonetheless. They would make their way through Northern Georgia then into Tennessee before hitting the interstate and heading to Kentucky. Wes's brother Will was two years older than him. Will was an environmental engineer and the two were close. Wes had no doubt that the authorities would be watching his brother's house so he had to be careful when contacting him. Will had no idea that his younger brother was working on such a large research project but he would be more than willing to help out in a time of need. Will was the one person in the world that Wes would trust with anything. He had an angle to play but he desperately needed his brother's help to pull it off.

The leaves were turning as the two made their way through the beautiful North Georgia Mountains. The smell of fall was in the air as the cool air refreshed them through small openings in the windows of the old Ford truck. Megan did not notice the picturesque setting. She stared at the road without saying a word. She was terrified, exhausted and she felt helpless.

"You have to believe that I am going to get you out of this" Wes said.

"My life is over either way. My parents are probably worried sick. All of my friends think that I am a cold blooded killer. There is no telling what types of rumors are being spread about me as we speak. Regardless of what happens, my life will never be the same again." Megan had a cold empty gaze as they rode and she spoke with no inflection in her voice. Reality had set in that there was no good way out.

"You don't deserve it. This is so unfair to you. I could shoot myself for even calling you to try to help me out. Megan, I am so sorry. I never meant to hurt you in any way. You are the first woman that I have ever really cared about. You are so beautiful, so smart and such a good person. This is the last thing that should ever happen to someone like you. If I could make it go away, I would."

"Maybe we should just turn ourselves in" she said. "We haven't done anything wrong and the longer that we run, the worse it is going to look."

"I've thought about it, I really have. The problem is that whoever set us up is really good at what they do. They will figure out a way to pin the murder weapon on us. Believe me, they don't want any holes. This needs to be an open and shut case for them. And I don't want to scare you, but I think if we get caught, we may never see a trial. I think we might be killed because of what we know."

Megan grabbed his hand and shuttered at the thought of what their future might hold.

"What is your brother like?" Megan asked in an attempt to get her mind off of the situation.

"He's a good guy. He is married with two daughters and he's two years older than me. I tortured him throughout our childhood but once we both went off to college, something changed. We have gotten along ever since. I regret the way that I treated him back then but there is nothing that I can do about it now. He is one of a very few people in this world that I can truly trust.. How about you? Do you have any brothers or sisters?"

"No, I'm the only child in my family. My parents wanted to have more kids but they couldn't. I'm really close to my dad. I am definitely a daddy's girl."

As they crossed the Kentucky line Wes pulled out the cell phone that he had bought at Walmart. He dialed Will's work number and on the third ring he answered.

"Will Holland"

"Will, hey it's Jason Johnson"

"I don't know anyone named Jason Johnson"

"Remember me? I'm Wes's friend from high school. Remember."

There was a pause on the phone.

"Oh yeah, Jason, I remember you. I'm sorry, it's been a crazy couple of days. What can I do for you?"

"I was just calling to tell you that I'm sorry to hear about Wes. There is no way that he did it. There has got to be an explanation."

"I'm sure that there is."

"Well I just wanted to let you know that I'm sorry. Hey, do you ever go hunting at the old lodge near your house that Will was telling me about?"

"Actually, I am going scouting for deer there tonight."

"Well, you should invite me up some time. I am a big hunter and I would love to see it."

"We will have to do that sometime. I appreciate your thinking about me."

Wes turned to Megan as he hung up the phone. "It's set. We will see him tonight and he has the old lodge that his company owns where we can crash for a few days."

"Are you sure that he knew it was you? That was about as vague as you can get?"

"I am positive. He will be there."

"What are you going to have him do?"

"I am going to have him pay a visit to Professor Michaels' wife. She knows me well and deep down I think she will know that I didn't murder her husband. If Will can get Harold Michaels' rolodex then we can start making some progress. He was very close with his wife and if anyone can help us, it's Sue. She is a sweetheart and I'm sure that she is destroyed right now. But she also knew that our project was his life's dream. That has got to stand for something."

The lodge was located deep in the woods near Lawrenceburg Kentucky where Will owned a small farm. It was a seldom used weekend retreat for the environmental engineering firm where he worked. Will had access to it at all times because he was the only real hunter in the company. A single light burned in the main living area when Wes and Megan pulled up.

As they got out of the truck and stretched their legs from the long drive, Wes took in the area around the lodge. They were deep into the country and there was not another house within miles. It was peaceful and quiet with the only sounds coming from the constant chirping of thousands of crickets and an occasional yelp from a bullfrog in the nearby pond. Wes breathed in the fresh air and knew that this was exactly where he needed to be for a good night's rest. The trauma of the past twenty four hours had really taken its toll and he needed some time with no one chasing him.

Wes also needed his big brother. Will always had a level head and was someone that he could always count on. His brother wouldn't judge him and would do anything that he could to get him out of the horrible situation that he was in.

"Where have you been hiding this place?" Wes asked. "It's like a redneck's Taj Mahal."

"Yes, it's pretty awesome" Will replied.

The lodge was two stories and made of cedar with vaulted ceilings in the main room. It had a game room, outdoor hot tub and would sleep twelve but was rarely used.

"Will, meet my girlfriend Megan."

"It is a pleasure" he replied.

"It's so good to see you" Wes said while giving his older brother a bigger hug than normal. "Are you sure that no one followed you?"

"I was very careful. Wes, what in the world have you gotten yourself into? You're on every major news channel and I've had three different visits from the cops."

33

"Well I didn't kill anybody and I plan on telling you the whole story but let us get settled in first."

Megan excused herself and went to take a long hot shower while Wes filled his brother in on his dilemma.

"Will, I would have never started this project if I had known this could happen. I just don't know what to do. I am panicking here man. Now Professor Michaels is dead and I've dragged Megan into it. She didn't even know about the project until yesterday. I just feel terrible about the whole thing. But I can't go back in time. The reality of this deal is staring me right in the face and I honestly don't know what to do. I'm stuck."

"You can stay here for as long as you want. I can bring you food and we will park your truck in the garage so no one can see it. I had my old truck painted and I switched the plates so if you need to go somewhere you can. We will figure this out Wes. We just need a little time."

"Thanks man. I knew that I could count on you. I will never be able to repay you for helping me through this."

"We're brothers, you can always count on me. I just don't know how we are going to get you out of this mess."

"Does Katherine know about you coming here?" Wes asked. He loved his sister in law and did not want to drag her into the mess in any way.

"She knows I'm here but she doesn't know that I've heard from you. I figure the less that she knows, the better. I hate lying to her but I feel like it's for her own good and the good of the girls."

"I agree. It's best that she doesn't know. Have you talked to mom and dad?"

"They are worried sick. They don't believe that you did anything wrong but they are worried about you."

"Tell them that I am fine. I hate putting them through this. I just can't believe that this is happening. Tell them that I will talk to them when I can but to please not worry."

"Yeah right, mom and dad worry when nothing is wrong so you only imagine how they are now. Wes, we've got to get to somebody on the inside of this thing. We need somebody important on our side. It's the only way out."

"We don't even know who is after me. We need to figure that out first. And it starts with Mrs. Michaels."

"She may not even talk to me. You are accused of killing her husband. Man, your girlfriend takes long showers" Will said.

"Let me check on her."

Wes saw the note at the exact same time as the spotlight from the helicopter shot through the front window of the lodge.

"Will, I've got to get out of here. Megan sold me out!"

Will had already seen the helicopter and knew exactly what was going on.

"Get downstairs now!" Will screamed.

The two brothers jumped four steps at a time to make their way from the main area of the lodge to the garage basement. Will went to work immediately by throwing the tarp off of a four wheeler and starting the engine.

"Get on the back. We will be driving blind but I know these woods like the back of my hand."

The loudspeaker on the chopper blared as Wes jumped on the back of the four wheeler. "This is a warning. The lodge is surrounded. Come out with your hands up."

Will opened the automatic garage door, gunned the engine and flew into the darkness of the intimidating forest with their heads just missing the opening door. If they passed someone as they darted out of the garage, Wes didn't see it. He didn't bother looking back to check either. His heart pounded as he closed his eyes, waiting for a gunshot to pierce the back of his head. He had never known what the moments before death were like until the past three days. He hated the sensation and would trade it for a boring life with no worries immediately if he could. He bear hugged his brother and hung on for dear life with his eyes closed as they weaved through the dark woods. Adrenaline rushes were overrated. When they were out of the distance of the lodge, they still had to worry about driving a four wheeler at night through woods with no lights. Will was a daredevil, he always had been.

"Slow it down, your going to get us killed" Wes pleaded.

"Look who's talking. Just shut up and let me drive."

After forty five minutes of taking hiking trails, Will pulled up to an old pick-up truck that was hidden in deep brush. An old logging road snaked its way to the main highway that led to Lexington.

"I took precautions" he said.

"Thanks big brother. Meet me at the farm in Belvidere in one week. And bring your laptop. I hope and pray that I haven't gotten you into any trouble."

"Don't worry about me. You take care of yourself and get out of here before they find you. As far as I'm concerned, I was scouting for deer when you must have arrived tonight. I had no idea you were coming."

"Thanks again"

"Don't worry about it. Now get going."

"One last thing, in case I don't show up look under our favorite dogwood tree at the farm. Under the rocks, you will find what you need. If something does happen to me, please get the contents of that box to Mrs. Michaels."

"Don't even talk like that. I will see you in a week."

CHAPTER 5

I put the keys into the ignition of the old 1970 F360 Ford pick-up and started down the logging road toward the highway. I had no idea where I was going or what was going to happen next but I was relieved that we had escaped. My brother had saved my butt and my girlfriend had turned on me. When the helicopter arrived at the lodge, I grabbed the note that Megan left before we ran. I turned on the interior light and read as I drove.

Wes,

I called my dad with your cell phone and in exchange for my freedom, I let them trace the call. I am so sorry but I had to be selfish. I hope that you understand and I apologize for ending things like this. I wish you the best of luck and I will tell the authorities that you are innocent. Take care of yourself.

Love,

Megan

That was that. I was starting to fall in love with her and hated that it ended the way that it did. Some good did come from it. She would be free, my guilt would be gone from dragging her into my problems and I could focus all of my attention on finding out who was setting me up. I didn't blame her for being selfish. In a lot of ways the act wasn't selfish at all. She was an innocent suspect cooperating with authorities. She was doing what she was supposed to do. She deserved a normal life and I hoped that some day she would find it. The downside to her leaving was completely selfish on my part. I loved her companionship and having someone to lean on. Being chased around the country wasn't easy but hiding alone was easier than hiding with someone else. I decided to pay a visit myself to Sue Michaels but I had a stop to make before seeing her.

Belvidere, Tennessee is a small farming community in the middle of the state. It was also the home of my grandparent's farm. My grandparents were no longer alive but I wanted to stop by the place to see if their old house was still standing. I had no idea who now owned the property but I needed to go somewhere peaceful so that I could collect my thoughts. The past three days had really taken a toll on me mentally and physically so I wanted to spend a few hours in a place that brought me so much happiness as a child.

As I pulled up the old driveway, everything looked much smaller than it did as a kid. The farmhouse that I thought was enormous was just a little house that was now falling down. It was beautiful as I remembered but you could tell that the grounds had not been maintained. I spent some time walking around the place. The old garden that had supplied the best dinners that I ever enjoyed was now just a clump of old weeds. The garage that had housed my grandparent's old truck had collapsed. The farm was a shell of its former self. But it brought back memories, great memories. It reminded me of times when all I had to worry about was what game I was going to play with my brother. It reminded me of what great people my grandparents had been. I always thought that they were rich when in reality they had little money. But they were rich in more important ways. There were always visitors coming and going from their house. No one left their house empty handed. They didn't have much to give, but they shared like no one I had ever met. They were truly happy because they realized that material possessions didn't matter. I could only hope to find their kind of happiness one day. I think that they would be proud of me. They changed their little piece of the world and now I was trying to change mine.

Before I left, I buried a very important disk under an old rock next to my favorite dogwood tree in their front yard. It was only a matter of time until my pursuers were going to catch up with me, so I placed the disk for the New World Project in the safest place that I knew.

When Will returned to the lodge, he was met by a small army. He casually drove the four wheeler up to the front door and lazily exited the vehicle, grabbing the tree stand that he picked up on the way back from dropping off his brother.

"Where is he?" a policeman barked as four others surrounded Will.

"Where is who?"

"You know damn well who. Where is your convict brother?"

"How should I know? You guys have been to my house three times already. I haven't seen Wes in quite some time. You know that."

"Do you want to go to jail tonight for obstructing justice?"

"Sir, I am not obstructing anything. You can search the lodge and search my house. I'm not hiding my brother. I came up here tonight to get away from you guys. My brother is out there somewhere and he's in trouble. I'm worried about him and all that you guys want to do is pester me. I want to find him as much as you do."

"Shut up you moron. His girlfriend was here just an hour ago and she called us. Stop lying and tell us where he is."

"Listen officer, I have spent the past three hours in a tree stand scouting deer. If Wes was here, I wasn't. If a girl was here, then I wasn't. If you want to arrest me, go ahead. But I haven't done anything wrong."

"We're watching you Holland. You make one wrong move and we will throw the book at you."

"Like I said, if you want to arrest me, do it now. Otherwise, I have a wife and family to go home to."

"You need to remember that son. You have a family and helping out your fugitive brother could get you into a lot of trouble."

"If I see him or talk to him, you will be the first to know."

I had no idea what I was going to say to Sue Michaels. I was so nervous about how she would react. She could call the police and have me arrested, she could slap me in the face and call me a killer or she could help me. It was self-ish of me to approach her less than a week after her husband died but he would have wanted me to get to the bottom of the problem.

Their house was in a beautiful area of Buckhead. Huge old oak trees lined the streets, every yard was perfectly manicured and every home had its own distinct look. The homes were built in the 1920's, when yards were large, profit was secondary to quality and uniqueness was the norm. It was the way that neighborhoods should look. To purchase a home like it today would cost a few million dollars in Atlanta. With the housing market in shambles, there were For Sale signs on almost half of the houses. The Michaels had purchased the home many years ago for two hundred fifty thousand dollars. It was paid for and they had no intention of moving. It was perfect for Professor Michaels. He had a ten minute commute to Georgia Tech and Sue had a large perfectly manicured yard to play in. I didn't know how to approach her so I just decided to go for it.

She answered on the third knock.

"Hello Sue. May I please come in?"

"Wes. What are you doing here?" She was shocked to see me. The man that murdered her husband was standing right in front of her. She looked ten years older than when I had seen her just a month before. The events of the past few days had taken a heavy toll on her.

"Sue, I need to talk to you. Can I please come in?"

"I don't have anything to say to you Wes. Now please leave."

Tears started flowing down my cheeks as I spoke. "Sue, I swear to you that I didn't do it. You know that it wasn't me. He was like a second father to me. You have to believe me."

She stared into my eyes for about thirty seconds without saying a word. "Pull your truck around back so that no one sees you."

"Thank you Sue."

We sat on her back patio that was lined with the most beautiful rose bushes that I had ever seen. She brought two ice cold glasses of lemonade and some homemade bread.

"Have you had anything to eat?" she asked.

"No ma'm. I haven't eaten much for the past few days."

"Well this bread is delicious and I will warm you up a plate of food. I have more than I could ever eat from the dinner after the funeral. Just give me a minute."

She brought out a plate filled with smoked ham, macaroni and cheese, three different types of casseroles, green beans and fried okra. It was exactly what my hungry stomach needed and I devoured every bite. It was her way of telling me that she believed me. We stayed silent as I ate, simply enjoying each other's company as we had done many times over the past three years.

"How are you holding up?" I asked while finishing a piece of chocolate cake.

"Not good Wes. I still just can't fathom this. I knew from the minute they accused you that you didn't do it. And I told the authorities from the beginning but they just didn't want to listen. They said that they had a witness that put you at Harold's office twenty minutes before it happened and they found a murder weapon that has your prints on it."

"No they don't. They may say that they do but they don't. I have never even held a gun in my life other than Will's shotguns. I hate them. They freak me out. Do you have any idea who could be behind this?"

"I have theories but nothing concrete."

"I don't know who it is but they are professionals. I was using the bathroom late on Saturday night when my hall mates woke me up and a team of assassins came to my dorm room. I jumped from the bathroom window on the third floor and I have been on the run ever since. I saw Harold's picture when I was trying to buy some supplies at a Walmart and it has all gone downhill from there."

"It is about the New World Project isn't it?"

"I'm afraid so. I knew that it would be controversial but I had no idea that anything like this would happen."

"You know Wes, this project was his crowning achievement. He was so proud of it and he was so proud of you. You two made an amazing team. He loved you like a son. He always wanted to change the world and you guys were about to do it."

"Sue, you and I have to continue this fight. Harold would be so mad at us if we didn't. I am more driven now than ever to make our dream come true."

"You have a long road to hoe before you can even go down that path. If my hunch is right, Harold's murder was ordered from way up the political ladder."

"How high?"

"Almost as high as it goes."

"So you think it was the government?"

"I think that it was someone in the government along with some other very powerful people."

"I'm screwed aren't I?"

"Language Wesley."

"I'm sorry Sue. Is there any way that you see me getting out of this?"

"I don't know. But I will give you all of the information that I have. Come with me to Harold's study. I have something to show you."

CHAPTER 6

"I'm so sorry to put all of this on you at a time like this" I said.

"Wes, I'm actually glad you came. I have a choice. I can sit around this house moping all day or I can help you avenge my husband's death. Harold would want me to work with you."

"Well I need all of the help that I can get and I knew that you were probably the only person that could do it."

"What I am about to show you is very high level information. It is highly classified and something that Harold made me swear to secrecy before he showed me. I am not showing you this to scare you but you need to know what you are up against. I believe that the group behind Harold's murder is a secret society known within high ranking political circles as Supero, which is the Latin word for dominant. Harold did not have a list of members but he had strong suspicions that he knew several members."

"What is the group's purpose?" I asked.

"The unofficial purpose of the group is to insure a disproportionate percentage of the world's wealth remain within its membership. To be considered for membership, you either must be among the wealthiest people in the world or have enough political power to influence major policy decisions."

"And how did Harold know this?"

"Harold is in the inner circle of many powerful men. Our current president was his roommate in college at MIT. He spent a lifetime working with high ranking government officials on projects that influenced technology and policy decisions all over the world. But your New World Project was his favorite. He never felt like he did anything to positively change the world that he lived in until you came along. You are a very special young man Wesley."

"Did he think the president was a member of Supero?"

"No. Not at all. President Davis is a good man with strong moral convictions. He and Harold had strong disagreements regarding their political views and in particular global warming, but the President is a good man. His problem is that he is too trusting and Harold never could convince him that people around him were corrupt."

Sue cleared her throat before continuing. "This group is very, very powerful. After the end of the Cold War, there was a meeting of twelve of the richest and most influential men in the world. They decided that to insure world peace, there needed to be a Secret Society formed that oversaw the world's economy. This group has so much money that they can manipulate the stock market however they see fit."

"What about the crash in 2008?"

"They made a mistake regarding the United States housing market. If you ask me, world peace is not at the center of their mission, greed is. The US housing market had rising values every year for decades. They were careless in allowing sub-prime mortgages to be offered and they paid the price. But if you think the financial bailout package was passed to help the economy recover, you are only partially right. Several of the members of Supero were heavily invested in the investment banks that were about to go belly up. So they saved themselves. The change has been very subtle in the United States, but Harold really felt like the group's agenda was to create two classes of people, an upper class and a lower class. The theory is that with money comes power so if the majority of wealth was only held by a few, then Supero would have more control over the people."

"This is crazy."

"Think about it Wes. Over the past decade thousand and thousands of good factory jobs have been exported overseas. Customer service jobs are heading in the same direction. Now accounting jobs, medical transcription and even some research and development work is being done in other countries. Corporate profit margins are up while those that were let go are having to find work elsewhere making less money in most cases. Profits have trickled up to the executive level and into the pockets of stock holders. The quality of product has gone down while profits have risen. And our political system is spinning this as a good thing."

"So slowly the middle class is being erased."

"Exactly. Some workers are smart enough to get retrained and make it in the new world but a lot of workers have jobs that they are overqualified for just to make ends meet. For all intensive purposes, we are just not manufacturing like we did in the past. We develop products and sell them but we do not manufacture them."

"Now some things are starting to make sense to me" Wes said. "Harold was adamant about giving manufacturers tax breaks on transporting goods with the New World Project if they added manufacturing jobs in the United States."

"He did not necessarily blame manufacturers for sending jobs overseas because if your competitors are doing it, you have to do it to survive. He did blame our government for not offering more incentive for companies to maintain their manufacturing base in our country. And Supero was at the heart of it all. They want companies to make and sell things more cheaply so that the people that lost their jobs can still purchase the cheaper goods. But by taking income out of the middle class, the people with money hold all of the power. My husband knew if we gave companies an incentive that they couldn't refuse by making it very inexpensive to transport their products around the country, manufacturing jobs would make a comeback."

"And the middle class would make a comeback also."

"Yes, Wesley you are correct."

"Why didn't Professor Michaels tell me about this?"

"He told you what he thought you needed to know. You have to understand that he spent a lifetime making the connections that he did. He wanted you focusing on designing a transportation system that would change the world. He saw it as his mission to do what needed to be done to have that system accepted by our government."

"If this group controls the world and he knew that they would be against it, then how in the world did he expect that the New World Project would ever be accepted?"

"He was hoping that his old buddy President Davis would step up and support him. He knew that if he could gain the support of the President, he could get it done. But President Davis wouldn't support the idea. Harold said that he was not a visionary. Harold tried many times to explain to the President that his legacy would forever be remembered if he changed the world by supporting us. But President Davis could never be convinced."

"Why? If you have a chance to change the world, why wouldn't he do it?"

"That question has a one word answer, oil. President Davis thinks oil is the way to go and his mind will never be changed."

"And why is that?"

"Because the man that he listens to the most is invested heavily in a huge oil company and has the President blinded by his way of thinking."

"The Vice President?

"Yes. Wayne Marks is an oil man through and through. He will always protect his own interests."

"Is Vice President Marks a member of Supero?"

"Harold believed that he is."

"And you think Supero killed your husband."

"Yes I do. I have no doubt in my mind that Wayne Marks was behind his murder. I think that President Davis shared your plan with Marks and the Vice President didn't want his empire to fall."

"So if that is true, then you think that the Vice President of the United States set me up for the murder of Professor Michaels."

"Yes, Wesley that is what I believe."

Wes buried his face in his hands and rubbed his eyes as the shocking revelation hit him hard. He wanted the truth and needed to hear the truth but he was beginning to feel like his survival was hopeless.

"Who else is in Supero?" Wes asked in a defeated tone.

"Harold built a list of who he speculated belonged in the group. There are two oil executives, two higher ups in the automotive industry, two computer executives, one investment banker, one Saudi, one entrepreneur from India, and one high ranking member of the Chinese government. There may be more members but that was the list that he started before he died."

"This is unbelievable. So basically, there are a dozen or so men that run the entire world. I just can't piece it together. There are a lot of rich people in this world. How can twelve men control everything?"

"They have a genius system. There are a lot of rich people in the world. And this group knows how to manipulate these people without them even knowing. The system is actually pretty simple. Each member has established relationships with the wealthiest people in the world. They know that wealth equals power. So policies are set up to insure that the wealthiest people maintain that wealth. And Supero knows that as long as they keep the rich getting richer, they can control them. They were behind the policies that launched the tech boom in the nineties. They were in the middle of de-regulating Wall Street and the banking industry in the eighties and nineties. And you can believe that they are the driving force behind sending all of our manufacturing jobs overseas. So you see, the rich get richer while the middle class dissipates. They do it quietly and the American people just sit back and watch it happen."

"Has anyone ever tried to stop them?"

"You don't stop them. You figure out how to work around them. Or you work with them. Those are the only two choices. These guys make the mafia look like pansies. They have entire armies on their side. They have total control."

"How do they get lawmakers to do what they want?"

"It's really simple. They bribe them very discreetly. Congressmen need to show their districts that they are working for them. So when Supero needs something done, they allow just enough pork barrel spending in each district to get the job done. And their policies pass every time. The vast majority of Congress doesn't even know that the secret society exists. The few that do, understand clearly that when an edict comes down from above, there does not need to be any backlash."

"And how long has this been going on?"

"For almost thirty years."

"So how do I work with Supero? That has got to be my only chance, right?"

"It depends Wesley. If you want the New World Project to continue, then you have no chance with them. If you want to destroy everything and forgot the project, then you can beg for mercy and maybe, just maybe they will let you live."

"So there is no way that you think they will work with me at any level with the project?"

"Wes, use your head. The New World Project is a transportation system that will end gasoline use in vehicles. The Vice President, oil executives and Saudi Arabian members would never let that happen. And if we give companies tax breaks to keep jobs in the United States, the Chinese will be livid. This group will do everything within their power to make sure this project never sees the light of day."

Wes walked around his mentor's study, staring at the stacks of old books. He was scared, intimidated, frustrated and exhausted. He had righted himself with Sue which was very important to him. But he was not expecting the bombshell that she had laid on him. He was way out of his league. He knew that there was corruption in government but he had no idea that it was at such a high level.

CHAPTER 7

"I came to this school to change the world. I came here to work with your husband. How can I in good faith go back on everything that I believe in? How can I let him down. We spent thousands of hours developing our transportation system. It will change the world for the better. People will have a better quality of life because of it. There will be no more car crashes. There will be no more mothers that have to wake up in the middle of the night and hear that their child was killed by a drunk driver. Our air quality will return to normal within a few years so there will be many less children with asthma. We can leave a clean planet for future generations to enjoy. This project will atone for the sins of the past. How can I let that go?"

"You could let it go because you want to live, because you want a family and because you want to live to see your thirtieth birthday. Wes, I will not blame you a bit if you let this go today. I will stand behind you no matter what your decision is."

"What would Harold do?"

"You are in a very different situation than my husband was in."

"That is not what I asked."

"Harold would not let his dream die. It was too important to him. When all is said and done, how many people can actually say that they changed the world for the better? It is a powerful reason to live."

"It's settled then. I'm not quitting. So how my dear lady, are we going to beat this super-powered secret society?"

"In my mind, there is only one way. And it will not be easy."

"Let me hear it."

"Our only hope is Daniel Worth."

"As in the presidential candidate Daniel Worth?"

"That is exactly who I mean. He has gained a lot of ground in the polls over the past two months. He is young, bright, open minded and the environment is a huge issue to him. He's not caught up in the good old boy network and this is just the type of issue that could catapult him into the lead for the 2016 election. He would have to play his cards right, but it can be done. Harold was planning on meeting with him next week. He thought that Senator Worth was our best chance at getting the New World Project off and running. Somehow, I think that Vice President Marks got wind of the meeting and that is why Harold was murdered."

"So it will be dangerous but it's our only shot."

"It will be very dangerous Wes. The bottom line is, you have to meet with Senator Worth without anyone knowing. And he will need to blindside everyone on Capitol Hill with his presentation of the New World Project to the country. Once it has been made public, then all bets are off. Supero would out themselves if they killed you or Senator Worth once the world knows about the technology."

"Let's say that I get this done and Senator Worth presents the idea to the public. Is there any way that we can pacify Supero? Is there some way that they can benefit from this so that I don't have to look over my shoulder for the rest of my life?"

"The auto makers will be fine if they change their business. They will be in the tram making business. Profits will not be as high as they once were but they can also scale back research and development. The computer people in Supero will be fine and the investment banker will be fine. But the oil men, the Chinese member, the Saudi member and the member from India are going to be livid. There is no way around it."

"Maybe once this happens, the society will lose some clout since most of them will be hit in the pocketbook. Maybe they go away."

"That is exactly what Harold was hoping. But my guess is that they won't go quietly."

"That's scary."

"I know."

Wes sat back with his hands behind his head and pondered on what he had been told. "How do we get in touch with Senator Worth?"

"You leave that up to me. I know the Senator and I will set up a meeting. You can stay here in the guest bedroom tonight and I will start working on the meeting in the morning."

I spent some time on the internet learning about the man that could save my project and my life. Senator Worth was from Charlotte, North Carolina and played football at UNC. He was forty nine years old, which was quite young for a presidential candidate. Senator Worth was one of two senators that were elected as independents. He was running on a platform of bringing a divided country together and he was gaining momentum by the day. He was bright, handsome and engaging. He was fiscally conservative but was willing to spend money when it was needed. He promised a balanced budget in year one of his term as president and was respected around the country for his stance on fiscal responsibility. He was too young to have sold his sole in Washington and he was benefiting from it. He was exactly the man that I needed in the oval office.

After the first good night's sleep since almost being abducted, I woke up to the smell of bacon and eggs, a delicacy for a college student.

"Good morning Wesley."

"Sue this smells fantastic but you didn't have to cook such a spread this morning."

"It's a habit. I always made breakfast for Harold before he went to work."

"Well it sure smells good."

The last thing that I remember was taking the trash out to the front of Mrs. Michael's driveway. I woke up locked in this cell. I don't know where I am, who took me or how long I've been here. The right side of my head is so sore that I can barely touch it. I'm stuck in a tiny green prison cell that is so small I can almost touch both sides when I spread my arms out. I've got a bed, a toilet and a sink but this place has got to be over one hundred years old. After about an hour of deliberation I raised the nerve to call out but no one answered. I'm here alone and it's so cold that I can see by breath. I've wrapped myself in my blanket. The lighting is dingy but I can see across the aisle that there are cells across the way just like mine. No one has brought me food or even walked by but I've only been awake for about two hours. Whoever is after me finally caught me. Given what happened to Professor Michael's, this probably isn't going to end well. I haven't heard the slightest sound since I woke up which is a very eerie feeling. I just pray that whoever caught me isn't going to let me starve to death.

Waiting is the hardest part. In one way, I dread whoever is going to interrogate me. But on the other hand, sitting here dreading the inevitable is almost as bad. I have never felt so lonely and helpless in my life. I've already examined every inch of my cell and there is no getting out. A single light bulb burns overhead but I have absolutely nothing to do. If this lasts much longer I will certainly drive myself crazy. I have already talked myself out of freaking out several times. I just wish I knew where I was.

I wish I had called my parents to talk to them one more time. They are such good people and they do not deserve to worry about where their son is. Hopefully Will let's them know that I am fine, but they will see right through his lie in a second. Mom's probably working at the bank right now, trying to get through the day but worrying herself to death. And dad is trying to focus on managing his sales force but I'm sure that the day to day issues that he has to deal with are nothing compared to what else is weighing on his mind. They worked so hard to get me to Georgia Tech. Because I am from Tennessee, the out of state tuition was astronomical. If it wasn't for an eighty percent academic scholarship, I never would have been able to attend.

I used to complain about my sleepy little hometown but I would give anything to be back in Tullahoma today. You see someone you know everywhere that you go. The atmosphere is friendly and the people are more laid back than in Atlanta. But no, I had to go to Georgia Tech and try to save the world. I can only hope now that the world tries to save me. Small town America is underrated. The crime is low in Tullahoma, if you try to get to know people they will make you feel like you belong and you have a sense of pride in where you live. Atlanta is made up of people from all over the country that wanted to escape their small town but they always seem to leave their sense of community behind. Poor Will is going to know that something happened to me when he arrives at our grandparent's farm. He will wait longer than he should, hoping that I show up. But he will be disappointed. He will do everything in his power to find me but he has no idea what he is up against. Sue will worry herself to death while knowing deep down that there is nothing that she can do. I'm in real trouble.

If I leave this world, I will do it with no real regrets. I just hope that if they kill me that it is quick and painless. I've been spinning a quarter on the floor for an hour. I checked the lock on my door and although it is old, it is getting the job done. There is no way that I am getting out of here on my own. I can see that there is a lever that opens several doors at once but it is about fifteen feet away. I can now imagine what prisoners in solitary confinement go through on a daily basis. How someone can even think about rehabilitating themselves in a solitary cell with no diversions is beyond me. You are a caged animal. The only thing that you have to play with is your mind. It is the only thing that can take you away from the hell that you are in. The walls seem to be closing in on me. I've tried running back and forth but the two steps each way don't calm me down. Pushups worked for a while until I was so tired that I couldn't continue. I ended up just giving up and lying on my hard, cold and moldy mattress. The ceiling is the same color as the walls, a dreary light green. This prison had to be awful when it was in use and it's even worse now. If I just had a book to read I would be fine or something to get my mind off of where I'm at.

I used to wish that I could just have some quiet time to myself. The idiots on my hall would never shut up. I had to go to the library for some peace and quiet and even there students spent more time looking for diversions to studying than actually learning. I would love to be bothered by that dorm noise now. I would be right there in the hall with them, just being an ordinary college student. I would even attend their parties and drink myself into oblivion if I could just turn back time. They weren't bad people, they were just being kids, trying to figure out themselves. I thought I had it all figured out. I was sure that if I created something that helped people out, everyone would love it and love me for inventing it. Man was I naïve. Building the system was the easy part. Maybe it's my small town upbringing but I had no idea that people could be so ruthless and greedy. Everyone loves money and power but killing and manipulating to get it is another story. I just don't understand how someone can enjoy money when they cheated to get it. Maybe they have convinced themselves that what they are doing is for the greater good but I will never understand it.

My country has stopped progressing because of greed and money. We used to be the best of the best. We were the world's innovators and that is how we dominated. Somewhere along the way, the rest of the world surpassed us and now we are trying desperately to hang on as the superpower but we are becoming a joke in a lot of ways. We aren't even playing with our own money anymore. I can't even imagine what my grandparent's generation would think about us now. We borrow money from countries that are not our allies so that we can maintain the appearance of being the best. And now we are crashing and burning. Our deficit is laughable. Professor Michael's and I developed something that is new and innovative that could actually get us back on track to getting out of the mess that we are in and he ends up dead and I'm stuck in some prison cell in God knows where. I'm getting pissed.

Someone with sense has got to listen to us. There comes a time when reality has got to set in. Even when you are printing your own money, there comes a point where you need to live on less than you make. Our country sets a bad example that going into debt is a good thing and then the people follow suit. Credit card debt is one of the dumbest things a person can get themselves into. People are buying cars that take them six years to pay off. When they finally do get the title, the car has one hundred thousand miles on it and it isn't worth anything. And then people let banks talk them into taking mortgages out on a house that they can't afford. We need an awakening in this country and we need it now. And we need the New World Project because it will create jobs, cut the cost of traveling in half and become a great source of tax income to get our country out of debt. How hard is that to understand?

CHAPTER 8

I heard the footsteps just as I was about to scream from my anger filled conversation with myself. They were coming down the hallway and butterflies appeared instantly in my stomach. It sounded like several people were walking toward me. I sat up on my bed and braced for what was about to come. I said a quick prayer that I would make it through the next few minutes alive. Three men in suits appeared along with a man in a black military uniform with a rifle.

"Mr. Holland" the leader said. He was in his early fifties with a full head of salt and pepper hair. He appeared to be in phenomenal shape and was very clean cut. He had a dark complexion and a mole on the side of his nose. And he wasn't smiling.

"Yes sir" I answered in the most intimidating voice that I could find.

"Do you know why you are here?"

"I have an idea."

"You are in a very difficult position Mr. Holland or may I call you Wes?"

"Wes is fine."

"You are wanted for murder and you have been running from the authorities for almost a week now."

"That's about right."

"I don't like people that run Mr. Holland."

"You know as well as I do that I didn't murder my mentor. And you know that I ran because someone was trying to kill me."

"Ah, you came right out and said it."

"What do you want from me?"

"You know what we want Wes. If you give us the disk, you can have your life back."

"Yeah right, just like Professor Michaels."

"Let me tell you something on the front end kid. If you don't cooperate with me today, you are going to suffer. You can make it hard on yourself or easy on yourself. It's your choice."

"Either way I end up dead."

"No. It doesn't have to be that way."

"Oh really. You expect me to believe that if I give you the disk and promise not to ever speak of my project that you are going to let me live?"

"Yes, it's that easy."

"You think I'm an idiot don't you?"

"If you keep talking to me this way, I know you're an idiot. You need to shut your mouth until you tell me where to find my disk."

"I was a college student just working on a project to help our country out. I did nothing wrong and people come to kill me. They kill my teacher and tell the world that I murdered him. Now you hit me over the head and throw me in jail. Can you put yourself in my shoes for just a minute and see how you would feel?"

"It's a raw deal kid. But you're too smart for your own good. I don't make the rules but I do enforce them. And I've been given full authority to do whatever I need to do to get this information out of you."

"By Supero?"

"It's none of your damn business who I'm working for."

"You don't need to answer. I know who it is. Our sweet little Vice President who loves taking photos with his wife and kids after church on Sundays."

The leader laughed. "You are full of piss and vinegar. Too bad it won't help you now. You should have kept running because when I'm through with you, you will be crying for your mommy."

"Can we at least sit down and talk rationally about this?"

"I'm not paid to talk rationally." The leader turned to one of his goons and said "Rough him up a little bit and then I'll check back."

My eyes widened when I heard what the man said. I thought he was bluffing but as the goon took off his jacket, I knew that I was in trouble. My stomach fell and I felt a little woozy. There was no where to run. The cell door opened as the broad shouldered muscle entered. I stepped back to the far wall of the cell as he pursued me.

"There is no where to run kid, take it like a man."

The goon was surprised when I landed the first punch right on his chin. I wasn't going down without a fight. The punch stunned him a bit but all that I did was wake him up.

"You're going to pay for that."

And pay I did. I had not been in a fist fight since I was eight years old and he beat me badly. After the first two punches I was ready to be put out of my misery. The first punch was to the gut and I doubled over in pain. But unfortunately that was just the beginning. He was a pro. There was not one punch that didn't hurt. He blackened both eyes, loosened a tooth, broke my nose and pounded my kidneys like a championship boxer breaks down a contender. I regretted throwing the first punch because he taught me a lesson. He went above and beyond what he was supposed to do. When it was over, I slumped on the floor, beaten down and bloodied. The cell door locked behind him when he left and it was then that I realized, he could just come do it again whenever he wanted. That was the torture of it all. I had absolutely no control unless I talked.

As a laid on the bed breathing heavily and trying to nurse my wounds, I contemplated on how much torture I could take. Would I get used to it, or was I going to reach a breaking point? And if I was eventually going to break, why go through all of the pain until I reached that point? After one beating, I was a lost soul. I was lying on the bed just trying to imagine what POW's had been through. How could they withstand day after day of this? It was beyond cruel. I just didn't know if I had the inner strength to get through it. Was it buried deep down inside me somewhere? Was I tough enough to stand up for what I believed in? And was I willing to die for it?

I passed out from a combination of exhaustion and defeat. I had never known what true fear was until that moment. True fear is knowing that something terrible is happening and having no control over the outcome. True fear is being stuck in a situation with no way out. True fear is knowing that you are probably going to die no matter what you do. I had to rack my brain to think of a plan and I had to do it quickly.

I always thought that my tolerance for pain was high, but I quickly realized that I had never experienced sustained pain over any period of time. The worst thing that I had ever endured was a dislocated shoulder. The pain was terrible but once the painkillers were inserted into my arm, it all went away. To be stuck in a prison cell after a severe beating was no fun at all. There was no medicine to relieve the aching and no nurse to attend to your every need. It's just you, lying there in agony and wondering when the next round would begin.

The leader appeared after giving me a couple of hours to recover. "Wes, are you ready to talk or are we going to have to punish you again?"

"Who are you working for?" I asked.

"You didn't answer the question Wes. Are you ready to hand over the disk or are we going to need to inflict more pain upon you? I am going to break your fingers this time."

Oh Lord. They were actually going to step up the torture.

"Can I at least have some time to think?"

"No."

"What assurances can you make me that I am going to live if I give you the information that you are looking for?"

"You have my word."

"Your word means nothing to me."

"Well that is all that you are going to get."

"Then you are wasting your breath."

"Break his fingers."

The goon was back and he didn't look happy. The leader walked away, the cell opened again and it was me, the goon and the military guy with the rifle. The goon brought in a small table and a briefcase. I watched intently as he opened the leather case. Inside he took out a small hammer and a rubber tube.

"Let's get this over with" he said.

There was no way out and I figured if I cooperated he might take it easy on me.

"What are you going to do to me?"

"You heard the man. I'm going to break your fingers."

"How many?"

"Two to start with. Do you have a preference?"

I couldn't believe that he just asked that. Do I have a preference? This was just another day at the office for this guy. He thinks I'm buying a stereo or something. What kind of nerve does this guy have? My preference is that I need to get out of this place now.

The goon looked like a surgeon taking out his instruments. He had definitely done this before. He pulled the small wooden table up next to where I was sitting and tied my left arm down to the table with the rubber tubing.

"Put out the first finger and I would suggest that you don't move or you could really get hurt."

"Can you please just do it fast?"

I stuck out my pinky finger, closed my eyes and looked away. I could hear him raise his arm into the air and he slammed the small metal hammer on my finger with a fierceness that would make any carpenter proud. I screamed in pain and my right arm grabbed the throbbing digit out of reflex. The goon's expression didn't change a bit. He stared at me with piercing brown eyes. The scar that ran down his left cheek moved when he formed an evil grin.

"Feels good don't it?" he asked while chuckling.

Something clicked in my brain with his laugh and I turned into a mad man. An evil grin appeared on my face also as I pushed the pain far into the recesses of my brain. My adrenaline pumped like I had never felt it before. My eyes hardened as I stared a hole straight into his skull.

"Yeah it feels good" I replied with a sinister voice that I didn't know I had. "Hit me harder. Hit me harder!" I shouted. "Yeah! Yeah! Yeah! Come on. Do it. Break more fingers" I pleaded while emphasizing every word. "Come on big boy. Punch me in the face."

My eyes were bulging out of my head as they stared straight into the eyes of the goon. "Rip those fingernails right out. Do it! Do it!" I then started laughing hysterically.

The goon was shocked. I had reached a breaking point but not the one that they were looking for. I had snapped and he actually looked uneasy being in the same room with me. He packed up his briefcase and left the cell by backing out. I would like to say that my plan had worked but it wasn't a plan at all. I really had snapped. I was ready for whatever they were willing to give me. And if I had one split second to attack someone, I would not hesitate to do it. I was looking for a fight.

The leader was smart because he gave me the rest of the night to simmer down. The guard even brought me a bowl of soup and a sandwich. I'm sure that he was frustrated because most citizens that he had to torture would spill their guts at the first sign of violence. But I was different. They killed my mentor and attacked me for no good reason. There is a time in every person's life where you either stand up and fight for what you believe in or you give up. I wasn't ready to give up yet. But I knew that I still needed to get out of there. I had to get myself out of the prison to have any hope of survival.

CHAPTER 9

The next morning brought a new type of torture. The guard arrived at my cell and to my surprise he opened the door.

"Let's go" he said.

"Are you releasing me?" I asked.

"Don't you wish. You're going to the hole."

He walked me down a long line of cells that were just like mine. We made our way through what used to be a dining hall and then took a left to head to another area of the prison. As we turned a corner, I knew exactly where we were.

"We are at Alcatraz?" I said in amazement.

"You're a real genius" the guard answered as the Golden Gate bridge was clearly visible through one of the open air windows.

"Why do you have me here?"

"So you can't escape and no one can hear you scream."

I couldn't believe where I was. The same prison that had housed the countries most notorious criminals was my new home. Al Capone stayed here. Alcatraz was closed in 2010 when the San Francisco economy hit rock bottom. The Federal government had plans to re-open the island but obviously they were making use of it in the meantime. I started to understand the frigid temperatures and cool air at all times of the day. I was only a mile from one of the largest cities in the country but it might as well have been one thousand miles because I was still stuck.

Sue Michaels was watching from her front window when Wes was abducted. She knew that it must have been Supero that took him because no authority contacted her. As far as local, state and even federal officials were concerned, Wes was still on the run. A tremendous amount of guilt overcame her as she watched him being pushed into a van and taken away. They must have been watching her home, knowing that there was a chance that Wes would visit. There was nothing that she could do. She was in her late sixties and had severe arthritis, but she felt shame anyway. It had been nice having Wes around. She had lived with Harold for forty years so it really helped to have someone around for part of her transition into becoming a widow. She had no children so she thought of Wes as kind of an adopted son.

His life was more important to her than the transportation project. She was determined to avenge her husband's death and see the project come to fruition but the young man's life took full priority over the project. The only member of Supero that she had ever met was Vice President Marks. She would get absolutely no where with him. She was sure that he had ordered the murder of her husband. The only other person in the world that she knew to go to was the President of the United States himself. She knew him well because they were old friends from college over forty years before. She was friendly with the first lady and she and her husband had been guests at the White House twice during his presidency. He and Harold were very close friends. While their political views differed, the President considered Harold among a very small group of people that he could really trust.

She didn't have the President's direct number but she knew that she could get through to the first lady. Francis Davis had called Sue after Harold's murder and sent a beautiful flower arrangement to the funeral. Francis had offered to do anything that she could and while most of the time those offerings were never fulfilled, Sue needed a favor and she didn't care who she needed to ask.

Sue dialed her cell phone.

"Francis, this is Sue Michaels."

"Sue, how are you holding up?"

"I'm making it Francis. It's a big change. When you live with someone for so long it is really unsettling when they aren't around any longer."

"I can't even imagine what it must be like for you. When things settle down, you need to come up to Washington for a weekend. We would love to have you."

"Well Francis, I actually need to visit with the President immediately. I have a big favor to ask of him."

"He is in Washington this week Sue. I'm sure he can carve out some time for you. Is something wrong?"

"Yes it is Francis. I need to talk to him. Would it be O.K. if I flew up in the morning?"

"We will have a car pick you up. Just call me back with your flight schedule and we will see you tomorrow."

"Thank you so much Francis. You are a good friend."

The guard threw me in the hole and slammed the door. I was in total darkness. There was no sliver of light peeking through a crack in the door. It was totally black. Your eyes never adjust to that type of darkness and I was beyond afraid. I was terrified. I felt around the small cell to try to at least get my bearings. It was completely empty with the exception of a small metal toilet that was dry. There was no bed, no pillow, no nothing. It was me, a toilet and a concrete box. For some ridiculous reason, I initially sat near the toilet and touched it every few minutes just to know that something was in the cell with me. My last cell was like the Hyatt compared to this place. The hole was where they put the worst of the worst. Inmates that were deemed incorrigible were made to stay in the darkened cells for extended periods of time. It was so miserable that there was a very good success rate of positive behavior after a stint in the hole because even the toughest men were broken there.

There was no concept of time in the hole. I had no idea if it was day or night and no concept of how much time had elapsed. My torturers knew that if violence didn't work, this probably would. It was a mental game that they were playing. It had a time tested track record of success and after a very short few minutes I knew that the tactic was probably going to work on me. I had finally reached a point in the other cell where I thought that I could handle their torture. I was learning to cope and adapt and I achieved a level of mental toughness that I thought would sustain me for a while. The hole had thrown me back to where I was when this started. I was just a scared kid with no way out.

I knew that I needed to play some kind of mind game to retain my sanity. Thank goodness I still had my quarter because it was a savior. I spent hours upon hours throwing the coin across the room into the darkness and then searched for it. It took my mind off of the situation that I was in and gave me something to focus on. It also made me a little more comfortable with my concrete entrapment. They controlled my body but they did not control my mind. I would toss the quarter over my head then immediately cover my ears and make noise so that I could not hear where it would land. Then the search would commence. I became an expert at spinning the quarter on the ground and picking it up in mid spin in the darkness with both thumbs.

My pinky ached from the pounding that it had taken from the hammer. I was sure that it was broken. I ripped off a piece of my shirt and wrapped in tightly around the wounded appendage to give it some semblance of support. I felt fortunate that the goon had stopped at one finger. My pinky was the sacrifice that had to be made. I was thrown into complete darkness but at least they were leaving me alone. I needed to use the time wisely. I had to devise a way to get off of the island.

Sue Michaels was treated like royalty upon arriving at the White House. She did have to go through the customary security screening but after being searched she was waited on hand and foot. She enjoyed catching up with her old friend Francis Davis. The First Lady was a good woman that spent her days working to end child poverty and leading programs to enhance early childhood education. Her husband's position as the leader of the free world did not change who she was. She believed that every person deserved a chance regardless of their background. She was a rock as the country was suffering through hard times and she was a role model for millions of women.

After spending a couple of hours reminiscing about old times, Sue was led to a room outside of the Oval Office.

"The President will see you now" a young male staff member announced.

"Mr. President, thank you for taking the time to see me."

"Sue, it is so good to see you. I am sorry to hear about Harold. He was a good man and a dear friend. The world lost one of the great ones."

"He was a good man. I already miss him more than you could know."

"Has there been any progress in finding the young man that did it?"

"Well John, that is really why I am here."

"What can I do for you Sue?"

"The young man that is accused of murdering my husband is innocent. I know it for a fact."

"What makes you believe that?"

"John, I am going to put you in an awkward situation but Harold was murdered by someone connected with the Supero group."

The President looked away as the words rolled off of Sue's mouth. She had no idea how he would react.

"I don't even know if that group truly exists. As you know, there have been rumors for years that such a group exists but I can not say for sure that it isn't a myth."

"You are the most powerful man in the world. We both know that it exists. I wasn't born yesterday John. Harold was killed because of the New World Project and you know it."

She had just come out and said it. She wasn't sure how she would portray her views to the President but she was proud that she had the strength to say exactly what she meant.

"Sue, you are grieving and you are angry. I completely understand that. You have every right to be upset right now. But don't you think that you need to spend some time getting over this tragedy and then we can talk? It's only been a week."

"John, I am not going to be able to grieve until I get to the bottom of this. Pinning the murder on the kid that helped him create the project was an easy way to make it go away. The young man didn't do it, I know that for a fact. And he was abducted at my house which was never reported. So whoever took Wes Holland is the same group that killed my husband. You are the only person in the world that can get to the bottom of this."

"There is nothing that I can do."

"Did you tell Vice President Marks about the project?"

"No I did not. Harold and I had three different meetings about the project over the last couple of years but I never told anyone about it. I promise you that."

"Why were you against it John?"

The President leaned back in his chair and thought about his response for a moment.

"The New World Project in concept is great. The air would be cleaner, people would travel more efficiently and the government would generate more tax money. But to make that concept a reality would destroy several industries that have been the backbone of this country for decades. Our economy would be in chaos during the transition and that was not a path that I was willing to go down given the state of our economy now. And I still do not believe that global warming is real. Our climate has gone through periodic warming periods throughout history."

"I never thought that I would see a day when you sold out. I am disappointed in you John. Whatever happened to the young man I knew that wanted to change the world?"

"Sue, you will never understand the situation that I am in. Every decision that I make has consequences. I could not embrace your husband's project because doing so would have put our entire economy at risk. And when our economy is at risk, so is our national security."

"Well I'm not going to sit here and argue with you about it. Do you have any idea who could have taken Wes Holland?"

"I have no idea whatsoever."

Sue left the White House with more questions than answers. She wanted to find Wes but the President was no help. The trip was a waste and she was disappointed. Her husband had always expressed his frustrations to her about the project. Now she was beginning to understand what he was up against. You can have the best idea in the world but if you can not convince the decision makers into your way of thinking it remained an idea. She was glad that Harold never entered politics. The maneuvering and posturing made her sick to her stomach. She never understood why anyone would change their belief system just to get ahead.

Two days after entering the hole, the door opened. I was blinded by the rays of light that attacked the darkened cell. I was starving as the one bowl of soup slid through a slot in the door was not enough to sustain me. I was disoriented as the darkness had taken its toll. I shielded my eyes as a guard entered the cell.

"Get up."

I tried but my legs were wobbly.

"I said get up" the guard repeated while grabbing me by the arm and pushing me up.

"Where are we going?"

I was taken to an enclosed room with one table and two chairs. The door was locked behind me and I waited. A bottle of water was left for me and I drank it too quickly, causing my stomach to throb in knotted pain. I didn't know what was next but I knew that I was almost at my breaking point. The leader entered the room, pleased at the progress his latest tactic had produced.

CHAPTER 10

"Wes, are you ready to end this now?"

"Yes, I'm ready."

"Good. Where is the disk?"

"I will take you to it but I have conditions."

"I never said that you could leave."

"If you want the disk, you will work with me. If not, just throw me back in the hole."

The leader was standing on the other side of the table away from Wes. It was an intimidation tactic to prove that he was in control.

"What are your conditions?"

"I will take you to the disk and I want a car at the location. I want your word that once the disk is in your hands that I will be free to go. I want a commitment that once you have the disk, you will leave me alone forever. I want this to be over."

"And do you think that I am stupid enough to think that you don't have other copies?"

"We formatted the disk so that no copies could be made. It was too important to risk someone getting their hands on it. You know that you can find me if you want to. I just need for this to be over."

The leader left the room as I stared straight ahead into space. The leader obviously wasn't the decision maker. He re-entered the room and sat across from me.

"The plane leaves in two hours. We will get you cleaned up and head out in an hour. We will give you a car when you hand over the disk. We will also commit to you that it ends here. But you need to know that if word of this is passed along to anyone, we will kill your family and then we will find you and kill you. Am I clear?"

"Yes."

There was an old house where the caretakers of the property used to live where I was allowed to take a hot shower. The scrapes burned as I cleaned them but it felt really good to get clean. They had a new set of clothes waiting for me and a male nurse attended to my wounds. They set my finger in a splint and doctored me up as best they could. As they walked to the boat that would take me to the mainland, I knew that it was now or never.

The guard never saw it coming. The knife that I had taken from the kitchen in the caretaker's house had been hidden in my pants and as the guard boarded the boat, I saw my opportunity. I inserted the knife keep into the guard's thigh and quickly grabbed the assault rifle as soon as the guard grabbed his leg. I turned and pointed the gun directly at the leader and his two partners. The male nurse immediately put his hands in the air. It only took a few seconds for the tide to turn and now I had five hostages.

"You, help him up" I shouted to the male nurse while nodding at the wounded guard.

"You three, lay down on the ground with your hands high above your head. If you make one move, I will kill you. Now!"

The leader and his two partners quickly obeyed as I carefully patted down each one, removing a total of four guns. I then patted down the wounded guard, finding nothing. I removed three cell phones, everyone's belt and all shoes. I then had the five line up in one line and they began the march back into the prison. I spread them out around the compound so that no one could speak to another. The leader went into the hole and I was happy to put him there.

"It's funny how things change isn't it" I said while laughing.

"You'll be dead within twenty four hours if I don't check in with my boss."

"Then I've got twenty four hours to break you" I replied. "Thanks for the warning."

With everyone safely tucked away in their cells, I made my way to the caretaker's house. I found some pasta and made spaghetti, a meal that I enjoyed with a view of the San Francisco skyline and the Golden Gate Bridge. I then took an hour long nap on a comfortable bed, a luxury that I never quite appreciated until then. I watched a little television and just as the sun was setting, I decided to call an old friend.

"Sue, hello it's Wes."

"Oh Wesley, it's so good to hear your voice."

"It is pretty good hearing yours too."

"Where are you?" she asked.

"The story is too long and too crazy to get into right now but I have five prisoners that are part of the group that took me. I'm going to try to find out who they are working for but I wanted to check with you to see if you have learned anything."

"I wish I had better news but I went all the way to Washington and came up empty. I met with the President and he was no help at all."

"Well thanks for trying. Let me see if I can get something out of these guys and I will get back with you."

"You be careful Wes."

I owed a phone call to my brother who I knew would be worried to death.

"Will, hey it's Wes."

"Thank God you are alive."

"I'm not going to talk long in case your phone is tapped but I wanted to let you know that I am fine. I'm still trying to prove my innocence and I will be back in touch with you when I can."

"Thanks for letting me know. I will pass everything along to mom and dad."

The time had come. I had to get information out of someone one way or another. I decided to start with the leader. I knew that the guy had the information that I needed but I also thought that he would be hard to break. It was a time to leave ethics outside and do what I had to do. If I ever planned on having a normal life again, I needed to know who was after me. I opened the door to the hole and faced my enemy. I threw the leader a chair.

"Sit"

"Wes, you need to think about what you are doing here. I can't help you if you don't let me. We were going to let you go and we can still work something out, but you need to listen to me."

"So you think I'm that stupid don't you? You really think that I was going to take you to the disk. You thought that I would turn over the one thing that is keeping me alive."

"Yes, I thought you were that stupid. You will die Wes. It's just a matter of when and how. And if you don't let me out of this cell, you will die a slow and painful death."

"Shut up and sit in the chair. Put your hands behind your back."

I proceeded to handcuff the leader with a pair of handcuffs that I found in the caretaker's house.

"Now it's my turn. What's your name?"

The leader didn't answer. I faced the man and stared straight into his eyes.

"I've got nothing to lose. You were going to kill me. I am going to get information out of you tonight. I don't know your torture tactics, but I am pretty creative. You are going to hurt. You are going to cry. And you are going to break. You can either tell me what I need to know now, or I will hurt you. Do you understand?"

"I don't know who I am working for. That is the truth. My company was con-tracted to catch you. I have been following orders from the time that we took you."

"Whose orders?"

"I don't know."

The first punch landed squarely on the guys left jaw.

"You're going to have to do better than that" the goon sneered.

"I'm only getting started" I replied as the anger starting building up inside of me.

I took a can of mace that I found in the house and sprayed it right into the leader's eyes. He cried out in pain as I watched, horrified at what I had just done but trying not to show it. I allowed the man to scream for about a minute before taking a damp washcloth and cleaning the burning area.

"That is just a glimpse of what I am going to do. I wanted to give you a taste."

"I don't know who I'm working for" the leader proclaimed again.

The next punch landed on the guy's nose, breaking it.

"That is not good enough. Is it Supero?"

"I don't know. I promise." The man's answers were getting more desperate as a hint of a crying whine was beginning to shake his voice.

"Tell me what you do know."

"I've never met with them in person. The up front money was wired to me from a bank in Switzerland. No one has ever given me a name. We were just told to follow instructions and the rest of the money would be wired when we were finished."

I didn't know if I believed the man or not so I slammed the door to the hole, leaving the man handcuffed and sitting in the chair writhing in pain. I then moved onto the goon that had delivered the torture. I had been looking forward to this. The goon was in a regular cell so I handcuffed him through the bars before opening the cell.

"Payback is hell buddy." I said while opening the goon's torture case.

"Listen man, I was only doing what they told me to do. It's my job."

"Well your job is risky. But I'll tell you what, tell me who you are working for and I won't touch you."

"That's the thing. I don't know who I'm working for. They just call us and tell us what to do. I swear it. We don't know the client."

"So you were hired by a group to get me?"

"Yes, I swear it."

"For some reason, I believe you."

"So will you leave me alone?"

"I told you that I wouldn't touch you if you told me who you were working for. You didn't tell me."

"But I don't know. Come on man."

"Listen, I'm a fair guy. Hold one finger out and I'm going to break it. Then I'm going to beat the living crap out of you. Then, we will be even."

I did as I said that I was going to do. I beat the goon senseless and then broke his pinky. Afterward, I didn't feel vindicated. I was just upset that I couldn't get any information out of him. I was free, but it was back to square one. The torture ended with the goon. I even made everyone dinner and served them in their cells. I moved the leader to a regular cell and retired to the caretaker home for the night. The next morning I served breakfast and met with the leader.

"I'm getting out of here today."

"What about us?"

"I'll give you enough food for a few days and then probably call the authorities in three or four days to let you out."

"When you say probably, you are going to call someone, right?"

"Honestly, I'm not sure yet."

"You guys were going to kill me so I don't know. If you gave me who you are working for, I would give you a break. But you haven't told me anything."

"I don't know for sure who it is but I do know something that can help you."

"What?"

"I know that there is going to be a private meeting in four days at the Hyatt in Orlando. Whoever I'm working for is meeting there. I swear to you that is all that I know."

"I'll tell you what I will do. I'm going to Orlando and if what you say is correct, I will call someone to let you guys out. If not, you are going to starve to death."

"Fair enough."

"I still have a couple of things for you. Is there any circumstance where you would have let me live?"

"No."

"That's what I thought. I just want to let you know that if we meet again, I'm going to kill you. I'm letting you live here today. You need to resign from this assignment."

I was unsure of how to drive the boat back to San Francisco. A canoe was my only experience. It wasn't brain surgery but it was tricky around the dock on the San Francisco side. I knew that I was still a man on the run but I had new life. I wasn't going to prove my innocence in a prison cell and the people that were after me would be incapacitated for at least a little while. I paid cash for a Greyhound bus ticket to Atlanta, called Sue to tell her that I was on the way and dumped the cell phone that I stole off of the leader at the first bus stop in Phoenix. I called my brother from a pay phone in Amarillo.

"What's up big brother?"

"Nothing compared to whatever you are up to."

"You know our friend we discussed you seeing? You need to pay a visit in two days."

"Stay safe Wes."

"I have a plan."

"Like I said, stay safe."

CHAPTER 11

A greyhound bus was about the most uncomfortable way that I could think of to travel across the country. I had a roller coaster feeling in my stomach after one hundred miles and the journey lasted for over two thousand. I caught up on much needed sleep and ate more than my share of food to make up for lost time. I had one shot to prove my innocence and I needed help to get it done. My plan would have to be flawless but I had to know who was behind my kidnapping. It was not going to be easy so I bought a notepad at a gas station in Dallas to plot my revenge.

Sue was so happy to see me that she almost made too much of a spectacle at the bus stop. She was glad that I was alive and it was also a relief to her that she didn't have a death on her conscience. She always acted the part of the quiet and polite wife of the professor but few people knew that she was a genius in her own right, happy to contribute to projects without the limelight that her husband basked in. I was glad to have her on my side. I need someone that had plotted assaults against political machines before and she fit the mold. She was Harold's most trusted confidant but it was intriguing to me that I never would have known her role in their partnership had he not died.

"Sue, I can honestly say that I have never been more happy to see someone in my life than I am to see you right now."

"Well thank you Wesley, I am overjoyed to see you also. You look like you have been through hell and back."

"Sue, I'm surprised to hear a semi cuss word out of you."

"Things change quickly Wesley."

"Don't I know it."

"I hope that you have a plan because I'm afraid that I haven't gotten anywhere" Sue admitted.

"I do have a plan and I need your brainpower to put the details together. I have also asked my brother to drive down from Kentucky because I need his connections to make it happen. Apparently there is a meeting in Orlando in two days and whoever is behind my abduction is going to be there."

"So the people that murdered my husband are meeting in Orlando then?"

"We're going to nail them Sue."

"We will if it is the last thing that I do."

"I rented a hotel room for you and your brother at a Hampton Inn off of I-285. It is under his wife's maiden name. He is going to be here in a couple of hours so I will drop you off and let you get cleaned up and then we can meet tonight. I will bring dinner over and then we can put a plan together."

"It's nice to be back. I was worried for a while that I wasn't going to make it."

"So was I. Seeing your face has made my day."

I spent an hour filling Will in on the details of my capture and ordeal. He wouldn't have believed me under any other circumstances.

"Your nine lives are almost up Wes. And you're still a wanted man."

"I know. If we don't bring an end to this soon, it isn't going to end well."

"I thought you were dead when you didn't show up in Tennessee."

I thought I was dead when I woke up from being caught. It is almost like someone else entered my body. I never thought that I could endure that kind of pain. And I surely never thought that I could torture someone. It was hard, but it wasn't that hard. It scares me a little bit. I really didn't mind hurting those guys."

"Wes, don't worry about it. They hurt you first. You had every right to do even more than you did. You did fine man. I'm proud of you."

"Not bad for a non-hunter huh?"

"Not bad at all. And by the way, you are making me miss the beginning of bow hunting season. We need to wrap this up, I have a buck with my name on it."

"You can rest assured that I will never be joining you in a tree stand. I have had all of the hunting that I can stand for one lifetime."

Sue arrived with beef fajitas and enchiladas from my favorite restaurant in mid-town Atlanta.

"You really are a saint aren't you?" I said.

"After what you have been through, this was the least that I could do."

"Well thank you Sue."

The Hampton Inn where Will and I were staying was a suite with two double beds. Sue and Will sat on the couch and I pulled up a chair where we began the process of putting a plan together for our enemy's meeting in Orlando.

I started the conversation. "I had a lot of time to think about this on the wonderful two thousand mile bus drive across the country. My first priority needs to be to clear my name. I need some type of evidence that Harold was murdered by this group and the only way that I think I can get that evidence is to some how have a presence at the meeting. I am very lucky that my old roommate at Georgia Tech is an electronics freak. It is his life. He is actually involved in a joint research project between Tech and the FBI to develop new state of the art wire taps and undetectable cameras."

"Can you trust him?" Will asked.

"I think that I can. We are pretty good friends and he knows how much I cared about Professor Michaels so I think that he will help me. The reason that I brought you here Will is because I'm hoping that your old friend that works for Hyatt can get me in the room the day before the meeting."

"Wes, he is a manager at the downtown Chicago location. I don't even talk to him much anymore. I'll see what I can do, but I wouldn't count on his help. What do you need from him anyway?"

"I need two things. First, I need for him to look in the reservations system and figure out what room the meeting is going to be in. If this group is as important as we think they are, there will be a large security detail around them. They will have to do a sweep of the room before the meeting. So Hyatt would know where the meeting is going to be. The second thing that I need is a universal room key card that will allow me to go in and plant the wires." "Isn't the meeting in two days?" Sue asked.

"Yes. We don't have a lot of time."

"Will, I need you to get on the phone with your friend today and have the card over-nighted to our hotel in Orlando. And I need to be in Orlando by tomorrow morning to figure this whole thing out."

"Wes, I'm feeling a lot of pressure here. My friend at the Hyatt is Scott Morgan, but we haven't even spoken in four or five years. I don't even know if he is working today. He's going to think I am crazy."

"Listen Will, if it works it works but I'm pretty desperate here. For us to pull this off, everything is going to have to go right. I know that it's a long shot but we have to try. Just make something up."

"And you need to get in touch with your room-mate."

"That is going to be my project today."

"Well what are we waiting for, let's go."

CHAPTER 12

Todd Vaughn looked like he was seeing a ghost when I entered my old dorm room. He didn't know if he should scream, wet his pants or welcome his old roomy back. I didn't wait to see what his reaction was going to be, so I put a finger to my lips to beg for his silence. Entering the dorm was easy as I had allowed my week old beard to grow and with the aide of a baseball cap pulled down low, I had gone unnoticed while entering the building and making the three floor climb to my old floor. There was some benefit to not being popular. You could also sometimes go unnoticed.

"Todd, I need your help."

My old roommate stared at me uneasily. He was a nervous type anyway but this was almost too much for him to handle. He glanced at the door to see if he could make it before I stopped him. The past week had been a long one for him. It certainly was not what he had signed up for when entering his junior year at Georgia Tech. His roommate was wanted for murder, he knew that a swat team had barged into his room late on a Saturday night and he had been questioned by police every day since his roommate had gone on the run.

"Listen, you have absolutely nothing to worry about" I said in an attempt to calm him down. "I would never hurt you and I promise you that I will not get you involved in anything that I have going on. Todd, I was set up. Harold Michaels and I were working on a very important project and there are people within our government that never wanted the public to find out about it. I have been through hell trying to prove my innocence. You know that I would never kill Professor Michaels, he was my mentor. All that I want to do is prove that I am innocent. You have to believe me."

"Wes, I do believe you. But I'm not going to put my life on the line for you. I'm sorry but I just can't do it. My parents want to pull me out and I have a good thing going here. I'm working on things that I never dreamed I would be able to do in college. If I get involved with whatever you have going on, then I risk losing everything. The FBI is already thinking about pulling me off of their project. It just wouldn't be fair."

"I understand" I replied in a defeated tone. "I just don't have anyone else to turn to. I have people trying to kill me and I didn't sign up for this either. I was working on a project that was going to change the world and my dumb ass thought that I could actually do it. Professor Michaels and I were trying to do a good thing for the American people and all that we got for it was him dead and me as good as dead. It's been a rough week."

Todd peered out of the window. He wanted to help his friend, but he also wanted this entire dreadful situation to just go away. To help Wes would make him an accomplice while ignoring his friend's plea for help might keep him in school and out of trouble. He felt Wes's pain and he believed that his friend was telling him the truth but he was not up for any more drama.

"Let me at least tell you what I need and then you can decide if you can help me or not."

"Fine, I will at least listen to what you have in mind."

"There is a meeting tomorrow at a hotel room in Orlando. The meeting is at 5:00 and the people that are after me are going to be there. For me to ever get out of this mess, I need proof that I am innocent. I am trying to get access to the room before the meeting but I need your help because I have got to plant surveillance equipment in the room. It is my only chance. No one is going to believe me unless I have concrete evidence that I am innocent. All that I need you to do is loan me the equipment, show me how to use it and then I will never ask you for anything ever again. You will be completely out of this mess. Will you do that for me please?"

"You have to promise me that if you get caught, my name will never come up."

"Is that a yes?"

"I will help you Wes. But after this favor, that's it. Don't ask me again."

"I need something that won't be detected in a sweep of the room."

"How many angles are you looking for?"

"I would love to plant three cameras with microphones if possible. But how do you find three hiding places that are that good?"

"It's easy Wes. You know that this is my expertise. I have cameras so small that you can be looking right at them and never know that they are there. We can plant one under a desk or table, one on the television and one on a telephone. I now have microphones that can pick up whispers clearly. If you can get into the room and plant my bugs without getting caught, you will pick up everything that is said at the meeting."

"You may be saving my life."

"I hope that I can. You are a genuinely good person Wes. You were a pretty good roommate too, which is the only reason why I am sticking my neck out for you."

"I am really sorry for what you have been through. It wasn't fair."

"It sounds like you got a lot more than you paid for too" Todd replied. "I hope that your project is worth it."

"At this point, I will take living for another fifty years. If we figure out a way to implement the project it will just be a bonus. I am so glad that my room-mate works hand in hand with the FBI."

Will Holland was nervous to call his old friend at the Hyatt. He and Scott Morgan had once been very good friends. They spent a lot of time partying together in college and played together on several intramural teams. Scott was a heck of a point guard back in the day. Life had gotten in the way of their friendship as spouses and children took the majority of both of their time. Will felt guilty for asking a favor from someone he hadn't spoken to in so long. But he loved his brother and knew that he would get over the guilt. He didn't know how to approach Scott so he just decided to go with his old faithful, the truth.

"Scott Morgan, how may I help you?"

"Scott, hey it's Will Holland from college. How are you?"

"Willy boy, how are you buddy? How long has it been?"

"Probably five years. I am doing great. And yourself?"

"I'm good, man. Scott, I feel guilty for even calling but I'm in a bind and a need to ask you a favor that borders on unethical."

"So I see that you haven't changed a bit" Scott joked. "What do you need Will?"

"Are you sitting down?"

"Do I need to be?"

"Maybe. My little brother was framed for a murder that he didn't commit. It's a long story but trust me, he didn't do it. He got himself caught up in a big hush, hush project that some very important people want to disappear. And they want to make him disappear. We know that this group is having a meeting tomorrow evening at the Hyatt in downtown Orlando. We need access to the room before they get there. He isn't going to hurt anyone or even confront them, but he wants to plant a bug in order to record their conversation so that he can prove his innocence."

"Why don't you ask for my first born too while your at it."

"I know that it's a lot Scott but it's my little brother. I have to do what I can to help him."

"Just tell me one thing Will, is he on the good side of this problem?"

"Oh yes. But he thinks that there may be a high ranking government official involved. It is crazy, crazy stuff."

"This violates everything that my position is supposed to stand for. If somebody gets hurt, then it is all on me."

"You have to trust me Scott, no one is getting hurt. As a matter of fact, if my brother shows his face to these people, he is as good as dead. There will be a big security detail. He couldn't get to them if he wanted to."

"Man you are putting me in an awkward situation. I've worked my way up the ladder for fifteen years. If I get caught, I'm done."

"I know, I know. And I feel so bad for calling you. I hate asking people for favors, especially since we haven't spoken in so long. If I was not completely desperate, I wouldn't be making this call right now. I can promise you this, if our plan works, justice will be served. My brother is totally the victim here. The poor guy has dedicated his entire life to projects that improve the quality of life but he has run into the wrong group on this one."

Scott closed his eyes and thought of what his wife would do to him if she knew that he was putting his career in jeopardy. "I love you Holland, you were always a good dude. Give me their names."

"Well, that is one of my problems. I don't know their names."

"Come on man. How can I help you if I don't know who they are?"

"I need you to look in the system and see if you can figure it out. The group is going to be between eight and twelve men and they are very high rollers. Some of the wealthiest men in the world."

"Let me take a look."

"We've got a big dinner catered in the Presidential Suite. The group name that is on the room reservation is The Coalition for World Peace. They have ten rooms reserved for the night."

"I think we have our group."

"The Coalition for World Peace doesn't sound like a bad group."

"It's a front."

"Here's the deal. I will rent you a room under my name. It will be complimentary. I'm friends with the manager in Orlando. He will leave an envelope in your room and the key will open every door in the hotel. It's a master. Just don't get crazy and start going places that you shouldn't."

"No worries, Scott. Thank you so much. If you ever need anything you let me know."

"I need my youth back. And how about sending me about a dozen of those sorority girls we used to chase around?"

"Whatever you need big man. Thank you."

CHAPTER 13

The downtown Orlando Hyatt was very impressive. The lobby included a huge atrium with palm trees scattered throughout. Will's friend set us up with a complimentary VIP suite that gave us more than enough room to spread out comfortably. We had an entire living area where we set up our surveillance equipment. The property had a gorgeous pool with multiple waterfalls. There were several restaurants to choose from but we would be confined to our room for fear of being spotted. Just as Scott had promised, we had an envelope with a master key inside. The group that we were spying on would be staying in the Presidential Suite on the Penthouse level. The master key would be needed to gain access to the floor. We arrived late on the night before the meeting and Scott told us that the Presidential Suite was unoccupied so we decided to go ahead and plant our equipment.

Will was going to install the cameras while I watched from our room to offer guidance. The Presidential suite was like an apartment. You entered through a hallway that led into the main living area. There were two bedrooms in the suite but we decided to install the surveillance devices in the main area. There was a large dining room table in the main living area so we set up one of the cameras to film the table. The second camera was set to record any movement around the couch and three chairs surrounding it. The third and final camera was planted to capture a picture of the entire room. Will and I used wireless headsets to communicate as he worked. I had a live video feed in our room to watch his every move. After planting the devices he tested the audio in several spots throughout the living area. The technology was amazing and ten minutes after entering, Will was back in our suite.

"Thank God that is over" he said. "Now I can breathe again."

"Now we wait."

"Who do you think will be there?" he asked.

"I have no idea, but if Harold was correct, the Vice President will be there. We may not know a lot of the others. I just hope this works."

The next day crawled by. We couldn't leave the room, our plan was in place so all that we could do was sit and wait. We watched a fight on The View, caught up on the world in sports by watching Sports Center for a couple of hours and played poker to pass the time. At noon, we finally saw life in the Presidential Suite.

"The security detail is in the room" I announced.

Three tough looking guys in suits scanned the room, looking for anything suspicious. The entire Penthouse level of the hotel was rented which Scott said was a bit unusual. We nervously watched our cameras while hoping that our devices would not be discovered. The three suits were all business and their thorough search took the better part of an hour. As I watched, I was amazed at how boring surveillance work was. You wait and wait for something to happen before finally getting a rush when any type of action occurred. I could only sit and hope that the 5:00 meeting would bring some much needed information on who these people were.

We called Sue after the sweep was complete to let her know that our plan was still in place and that we would contact her after the meeting. She wanted to be with us but we didn't want her anywhere around should something go wrong.

She wanted to help but she also knew that she would be a problem if we needed to escape quickly. The catering crew arrived at 4:00 with a spread that looked like it could feed fifty. Security watched their every move as the group diligently went about their work. The crew appeared to be a bit on edge, knowing that the client they were preparing the food for was not the ordinary family going to Disney World. These people were obviously important. It was not every day that bodyguards watched them work.

The weather was terrific as we watched group after group tee off on hole number ten at the Grand Cypress golf course that connected with the hotel. I was jealous as I watched the golfers enjoy themselves. All that they had to worry about was keeping their ball in the fairway. Life was just unfair.

When the 5:00 hour arrived, we spread out on the couch, watching the computer screen in front of us. My nerves were fried as I gripped the pen and note pad that I would use to take notes. Will had his laptop beside him and had done an internet search on the world's wealthiest people so that we could try to piece together who we were looking at. The food was prepared, ten place settings were ready to be used and a freshly carved ice sculpture was the centerpiece of the massive dining room table. Additional security arrived although it appeared that the new guards were of foreign descent. At around ten minutes after the hour, the members finally started arriving.

As the guests filtered into the room, Will started identifying them. After only ten minutes, we were sure that the group that we were spying on was Supero. There were no introductory rituals or ceremonies needed for induction. There were only two requirements, you either needed to be filthy rich or have the ability to make others extremely wealthy. Everyone in the room fit the bill. We were surprised at the relative youth in the room. Only a handful of members appeared to be over sixty. We were looking at the most exclusive club in the world. A large percentage of the world's wealth was arriving and the mountain that I had to climb was only getting higher.

Dave Nelson was the first person that Will identified through the assistance of the world wide web. Dave didn't look a day over forty. He was an entrepreneur that made a fortune during the internet boom. He looked more like a surfer than an astute businessman. He was worth over two billion dollars and had spent most of the past few years enjoying his vast fortune. He owned a major league baseball team, was the proud owner of the world's largest yacht and was passionate about adventure racing. He was single and not in the market for a wife. I never would have believed that an earthy looking computer nerd would have been a member of the secret society that determined the way that the world worked.

Bob Blanton was the second man that entered the room. Bob was an oil tycoon from Texas and he was proud of it. He wore a large white cowboy hat, rattlesnake boots and a belt buckle that was bigger than most shoes. Bob appeared to be about fifty years old. He was a third generation oil man. His family owned oil rights all over the state of Texas. His central focus over the past year centered around some large natural gas pockets that were discovered in the Fort Worth area. The Blanton family controlled the oil business in Texas and there was a very good chance that he was behind my abduction and Professor Michael's murder. His vast fortune would be ruined if the New World Project ever became a reality.

Our third discovery was a man named Phil James. Mr. James was the CEO of World Airlines. World Airlines had taken advantage of the failures of other airlines throughout the recent recession. They had purchased three major airlines over the past three years to form what many called a monopoly in the airline industry. No one understood how the government allowed all three takeovers but now I understood completely. The new huge company was on a roll and appeared to be unstoppable as smaller regional carriers were trying to reinvent themselves just to survive. The government claimed to have allowed the acquisitions because it was determined that it was the only way for air travel as we knew it to survive. Little did anyone know that the decision was made in a room of non lawmakers.

Criminal number four was Fahim al Zahrani, the oldest son of the wealthiest family in Saudi Arabia. Zahrani was educated in the United States, getting a degree in business and economics from Harvard. He lived in a palace, paid for with oil money largely from the United States. His family, along with a few select others, controlled the price of oil around the world. He had the power to move our stock market based upon the price of a barrel of oil. They were master decision makers, knowing the exact buying patterns of the American public. Prices always rose during the summer months and around holidays while they lowered prices during tough economic times. The business was always profitable, it was just a matter of how profitable. Zahrani could certainly be behind my troubles. His family had the money and influence to come after me and they also had a lot at stake. But the main question was, how would they even know about my project?

The fifth member of the contingent arrived in full military garb. His name was Jun Wu and he was the Minister of Commerce for the Chinese government. Wu was certainly one of the most powerful men in the world. He was the driving force behind opening up the Chinese labor markets to manufacture goods for companies all over the world. His country was attaining wealth at an alarming rate although workers were not seeing much of the profit. The Chinese people were quickly gaining ground on the United States in terms of technology. It was no longer a country only supplying labor. China had positioned itself to become the world power sometime over the next two decades. Professor Michaels had written in depth on the subject and truly believed that if the United States did not reverse course in several areas, China would become the new world power within his lifetime.

The next man to enter the room was Bill Douglas. Mr. Douglas was a retired auto executive and was the man who called the shots in Detroit. When the auto industry tanked, Douglas stepped in to take the lead and became the spokesperson for the big three. He admitted that the Asian manufacturers produced a better product and it was his last mission in life to turn the tide back to the United States. Douglas was in his mid sixties and had a no nonsense air about him. He was on marriage number four to a woman half his age and was trying desperately to hold onto his youth. He was proud of the very unimpressive hair plugs that he recently had installed and enjoyed the booze, scotch was his liquor of choice.

Jeff Bates was next. Bates was an extremely wealthy investment banker that had been under fire ever since the Wall Street bailouts. Bates was young, maybe forty, and had taken the world by storm through hard work, a brilliant mind and unregulated rules that made someone as bright as himself very dangerous. He knew how to bend rules better than anyone and there was not a financial loophole that he didn't take advantage of. Bates was the prime example of why the United States economy tanked in 2008. He was too smart for his own good and the country had paid for it.

Walter Phelps entered the meeting room with Bates. Will did not need to look Phelps up on the internet. He was the wealthiest man in the country. He owned over fifty of the most recognized brands in the world. He owned a little piece of everything and his track record was impeccable. He was praised throughout the recession for his company's track record during the tough economic downturn. He was over sixty but didn't look a day over forty. Phelps combined basic financial principals with sound decision making to build his empire. He started with nothing and was the poster boy for living the American dream. I was very surprised and disappointed to see him arrive at this meeting. I always thought that he was legitimate. He certainly had me fooled.

The men milled about the room, ordered drinks from the bartender, snacked on the appetizers and warmly greeted each other. They were all proud to be members of this exclusive club. Power was king and they held more power than anyone could ever have imagined. The final member to arrive was the most disturbing of all.

CHAPTER 14

"Oh no" I said as the final member entered the room. I stared at the screen in a state of shock.

"Is that who I think it is?" Will asked, unable to believe what was clearly in front of him.

"I'm afraid so" as all of the hope that I was feeling left immediately.

"That's not good at all."

The last member of Supero was none other than John Davis, the President of the United States. It was he who had murdered Professor Michaels, his good friend and former college roommate. Word of the New World Project had not been leaked, it had been shared with the enemy. There was no doubt that everyone in the room knew about the project. And if the group voted diplomatically, then they had voted to make my project disappear. The one person that Harold Michaels had confided in was the one person that he should not have. The most powerful man in the world was the leader of the most powerful secret society in the world. John Davis was a sell out. Greed had compromised many men and he was no exception.

Sue Michaels had explained to me that her husband knew his friend had changed, but obviously he did not realize the extent. Sue had even gone to the

White House to try to expose the conspiracy and was unsure why her pleas had fallen on deaf ears. Now she would know. Professor Michaels would have been so disappointed in his friend and he also would be frustrated at his inability to figure out that his friend was sleeping with the enemy. My journey to prove my innocence had taken a very difficult and probably fatal turn for the worse. As President Davis worked the room to greet his comrades I fought the urge to puke.

Drinks were flowing and the atmosphere was festive as the group joked and conversed for the better part of two hours. They were in no hurry to get down to business as the world literally revolved around them. Time was of no concern. It appeared to Will and I that President Davis was the leader of the group but there did not appear to be any real pecking order. We guessed that they all had equal power and age appeared to be of no consequence. Each man brought a unique benefit to the group. Each member controlled a certain part of the world which was what made the collective group so effective. Each was an expert in their field and had the final say of how their piece of the equation would benefit the group. We had no idea of the extent to which they controlled the world but we hoped to learn from their meeting. We would in fact learn what we needed to know and when all was said and done, we wished that we never knew.

When every dessert was finished and every glass was full, the wait staff exited and the mood in the room changed immediately. The security detail excused themselves to the hallway and the curtains to the suite were drawn closed. We were about to witness a meeting that countries would pay billions to witness. The exclusive society that had remained secretive for decades was finally being exposed to two nobodies that would certainly die immediately if the membership were aware of their presence. It was a small victory for me, even if it didn't change my fate. President Davis was seated at the head of the table and he started the meeting.

"Gentlemen, I want to welcome everyone here this evening. That was a wonderful meal and it pleases me to find everyone in such good health. We have a lot to talk about tonight so I thought we would begin with the war in Iraq. We are closing in on the ten year mark and it's time to bring our soldiers home. I realize that the conflict has brought us each a great financial windfall, but I can not fool the American public any longer. And I also have an election to win. If we pull out completely over the next year, it will secure my bid for re-election, which we all know would be a good thing for our cause. We will maintain the war budget throughout until our men and women are home but enjoy these last few months because this money is drying up."

Dave Nelson, the young internet entrepreneur, spoke up. "Mr. President, I knew that this day would come. I just want to personally thank you for what you have done for me personally and for everyone in this group. Fifty million a month for each of us is an amazing number. Who do we invade next?" he joked while laughing.

"I appreciate your good words Mr. Nelson" the president replied. "This war has been great for our pockets but it's time for me to get re-elected."

"Mr. President" the Chinese Minister said. "Do you have a plan to generate income for the group after you have removed your troops from Iraq?"

"Jun, I do have a plan, but the money will come from several different areas. The Defense budget will make up the lion's share, but I will make every effort to contribute up to ten million per month for each of you."

"That is more than fair Mr. President" Jun Wu replied.

"Mr. Wu, why don't you take the floor next."

The Chinese Minister of Commerce stood as he spoke. "Gentlemen, our exports have stabilized over the past year. We did take a hit initially during the recession but after the initial shock, we have rebounded quite nicely. You will each receive thirty million this month and we feel that we will be able to sustain this figure throughout the next year."

Will and I sat on the couch with our mouths open wide. We could not believe what we were seeing and hearing. This was scandal at its finest. I was starting to figure out exactly what the group was about.

President Davis remained the moderator. "Fahim, you can be next."

The wealthy Saudi stood to address the group. He was dressed in a suit which was not his customary wardrobe. "Men, we have decided to remain aggressive with the price of oil. We feel that the American public will travel less if we raise prices at this time. We will continue to spike costs during peak travel times, but oil prices will remain low except for the summer and holiday seasons. Until the world pulls out of the current recession, we will maintain this strategy. Given this fact, we will only be able to contribute fifteen million to each of you this month."

As the Saudi Arabian member of Supero sat back down in his chair, I wrote his financial contribution down on a piece of paper. Each member was already up to ninety five million each for the month!

"Mr. Blanton, you are up" the President said.

The oil man from Texas adjusted his cowboy hat, pulled up his pants and stood as he spoke. "Well gentlemen, as Mr. Zahrani just said, oil prices need to remain at their current level. Profits will increase for each of us when we pull out of this recession. I wanted to update you all on my latest endeavor, natural gas. We have found some really strong pockets in Texas, but obviously Alaska is where the money really is. We hope to have that pipeline fully operational within the next year and when we do, my contribution will increase dramatically. We are going to be able to contribute ten million to each of you this month."

"Walter, why don't you take the floor next."

America's wealthiest man remained seated as he spoke and pulled out ten reports from his briefcase, passing them around the room. "Men, I have a list

of twenty good buys this month. As you all know, we have all become tremen-
dously wealthy over the past four years by finding great bargains and purchasing
these stocks when they are at their low point. You have also done a great service
to these companies by stabilizing them through your stock purchases. I believe
that we will be in a buyer's market for the next six months and then my list
will shorten dramatically as the investments that we have made will reach their
potential. We will then become sellers. As you can see on the list, this month
I am recommending twenty stocks to purchase and six to sell. Thank you for
your trust."

The President spoke up "Walter, we would also like to thank you. You have
been dead on every month and we have all benefited. Keep up the good work."

As the meeting went on, I realized that every member had a purpose. Jeff
Bates, the investment banker, was in charge of hiding everyone's money. Phil
James, the airline executive, arranged travel all around the world for the group.
He also contributed with a monthly financial gift. Bill Douglas, the auto executive, provided vehicles to every member and contributed financially on the part
of the American auto industry. Dave Nelson, the entrepreneur, contributed
to the group by finding new start-up technology companies for them to invest
heavily in. When all was said and done, each member received one hundred
twenty five million each for the month. That equated to $1.5 billion each year.
The President's salary was four hundred thousand each year which was only
meal money compared to what he was really getting. Will and I were speechless.
We had no earthly idea that we would learn anything this staggering.

When the contribution portion of the meeting ended, they turned to other
matters.

"We will now address problems" the President said. "India remains a threat
to us. I have been unable to convince the Indian leader to join our group. I have
been very vague with him other than saying that it would be in his best interest to join. He will pay for his reluctance. I have been working with Mr. Wu.

China will now become a major outsourcer for customer service. We will heavily tax American companies that do business with India and we will put measures into place that slow down any and all business with the country. We will effectively put them out of business. This will be good for us all."

"The next topic is poverty level. As you know, the income disparity level within the United States has been growing at a tremendous rate. The plan is working. But we need to invest in the people a bit for a couple of reasons. First, we need a little more expendable income so that our people will continue consuming goods at their current rate. Secondly, I have an election to win and I have to pull us out of this recession to have a chance. Keeping the price of oil low is a good start. If we continue to buy Walter's stock suggestions heavily, that will help ease any tension on Wall Street. And we need to adjust the earnings reports for every major retailer so that everyone feels like our economy is rebounding. In short, we have pushed the envelope enough for now. We have widened the income gap between the upper and middle class. Now we need to ease back a bit so that people feel comfortable again and will start spending. It is a delicate balancing act. The economy can rebound now and we will have achieved the income disparity that we wanted when we started this recession. But it is time to grow and make some money. Are we all in agreement?"

Every member of Supero voted that yes, the recession should be over.

"Good then, it's settled. The recession ends now. We will allow stock prices to climb. That will ease the population's fear and their 401K's will start rebounding. We will get bank's to loosen their belts and start loaning again. And companies will start adding jobs again. I must say that our plan was genius. It was painful for the American people, but it was genius."

"A toast to the middle class" Walter Phelps said.

"You should be toasting them Walter, you made more money on this recession than anybody" the young entrepreneur Dave Nelson proclaimed.

"We all made money on this recession" the investment banker Jeff Bates added. "It was genius. And by my calculations, the top one percent of earn- ers accumulated an additional five percent of the country's wealth during this period. We accomplished exactly what we set out to do."

"The poor bastards will never even know what happened. I love it" the big Texan Bob Blanton said. "Capitalism at its finest."

"In all seriousness, we must remember the purpose of this group" the President said. "At the end of the Cold War, this group was formed to oversee the world's economy. It was determined that by having a central group that controlled the economy, we could oversee the population. They would never realize that it is in their best interest, but we all know that it is. As long as we stick together and continue down the road of wealth disparity, we will control the world. A sharing of wealth is healthy to an extent as long as it is controlled. Wealth is power and we are in power today."

Clapping erupted around the room as the group reveled in their accom- plishments. Will and I had not moved, still unable to fathom what we were see- ing. The group really was controlling the world. Professor Michaels was dead on in his assessment. It was a sickening view but they were in control.

Chapter 15

The group took a five minute bathroom break before resuming their meeting which gave Will and I a chance to talk. My brother looked at me with fire in his eyes.

"Can you believe what we just witnessed?" he said.

"A week ago I would have said no but now nothing surprises me."

"I had no idea anything like this was possible."

"I'm just dumbfounded. I don't see any way that I can get out of this."

"What? Did the beating you took knock the sense out of you?"

"What are you talking about?" I said.

"Wes, we are taping this. All of it. You have dirt like no one ever could dream of. You have leverage brother, leverage."

"Yeah, you're right. I knew I brought you here for a reason."

"These idiots are getting rich by skimming off of the top of every major industry in the world. I knew that the war was costing ten billion a month and six hundred million a month is going straight into their pockets. How in the world can this happen?"

"Very smart accountants" I replied.

"And there is no system of checks and balances. This is just crazy. And to say that the spreading of wealth should be controlled is nuts. They are walking on very shaky ground."

"Will, this group only cares about themselves. They may say that they have the American people in mind, but this is about money and greed, end of story."

"The President is crazy. He is putting his faith in China and Saudi Arabia? Give me a break. You're right, it is about greed."

I sat back and thought for a moment. "Professor Michaels' ideas were doomed from the beginning. The President saw him as a threat to his own wealth and decided to take him out."

"And he's trying to take you out."

"Thanks for reminding me."

"Wes, let's just get out of here now. This entire thing is giving me the creeps. We have more than enough dirt on Supero to nail them. I'm ready to leave now."

"I'm not going anywhere. We are not leaving this room until that entire group is gone. There is security all over this building. If someone recognizes me, I'm screwed. The safest place for us to be is right here."

"I don't feel safe."

"They can't see us you moron. "

"I know that. I'm not an idiot. But the people that are trying to kill you are in this building right now. That has to scare you some."

"Well yeah. Of course it does. But it would scare me even more if we tried to leave right now. I want to hear what else they have to say anyway. We are already here. We might as well watch the rest."

The five minute bathroom break turned into fifteen but eventually they were all seated once again and ready to resume setting the direction of the world. Will and I resumed our positions after taking a couple of minutes to stretch our legs. I had to flip the page on my notepad. I was writing much more than I ever had intended. And unfortunately, I wasn't finished.

"Next on the agenda is what I like to call Shock and Awe. We have not discussed this topic in almost a year but now that we have decided to ease the world out of recession, we need something to maintain a feeling of fear in the American public. As you may recall, our last Shock and Awe project was bird flu and I must commend Mr. Wu for doing an excellent job. It was a tremendous scare tactic although it was fairly short lived. Right now we are in the heart of flu season here in the United States and I'm thinking that we need to release a stronger strain than normal this year. We need to release something that the vaccine is not effective against. That will certainly peak concern around the country."

The first dissention of the meeting occurred when Jeff Bates, the investment banker spoke up. "Explain to me again why we need to do something like this?"

The President appeared to be a bit agitated. "Jeff, a vulnerable group is easily swayed. It is much easier to lead people in the face of crisis. The population will rally around leadership when times are uncertain as long as the leadership provides a sound plan and a strong and steady demeanor. It is a proven fact."

"I'm sorry Mr. President. I'll be honest, influenza scares me. I've got three small children and it certainly worries me."

"Jeff, should we decide to release a deadlier strain of influenza this year, your family along with the immediate families of everyone in this room will receive a vaccine. Your family will not know it, but they will receive a different vaccine than the rest of the country."

"Thank you sir."

"Are there any other questions or concerns?"

Bill Douglas, the former auto executive and current Detroit spokesperson spoke up. "Mr. President, why mess around with an influenza virus. If you really want the people to rally around you before an election, why not pull off another terrorist attack on American soil?"

"Well Bill, that is actually the next item on my list."

Will looked over at me once again. When we thought that we had heard it all, the group just kept on shocking us. We could not comprehend what we were hearing. The President looked around the room and then began speaking.

"If we really want to reign in the American people and get their thoughts off of the economic downturn, a terrorist attack is the best way to do it. Daniel Worth is my running mate for the next election. He is young, inexperienced in foreign affairs and there is absolutely no way that the American public would elect him if they felt that our homeland was vulnerable. To do this would seal the next election for me."

Bob Blanton, the Texan, spoke up. "President Davis, do you think that the economy could take another hit that an attack would cause? I may sound greedy here but the price of oil is low enough already."

"Bob, I hear what you are saying but if the attack occurs away from New York City, I think that we can convince the public to rally through tough times.

I think the markets would take a big hit for a couple of days after the attack, but after that I believe that we would see the rally that we need to get us out of this recession. Jeff, you're the banker, what are your thoughts?"

Jeff Bates looked nervous. He was the newest member of Supero and was still getting used to the scale of the decisions that the group made. He still valued human life but he also knew that to blink in front of this panel would get him killed. "The President is correct. The markets most likely would rally within a week after the attack. The pride of the American people would shine through and it would most likely pull us out of the recession a bit faster than if we simply allowed it to happen naturally."

Walter Phelps spoke next. "Mr. President, do you feel like we need to make this happen for you to secure a second term?"

"Senator Worth is gaining ground every month. He's got liberals, young voters, the black vote and a lot of women on both sides of the aisle. The thing that has me nervous is that he is swinging independents in alarming numbers. People are tired of the war and they want the economy to rebound. If I announce a plan to pull all of our troops out over the next year and we put an end to the recession like we discussed earlier, I will probably win the election. But the only sure way is to attack the homeland."

"Then let's do it" Phelps said without flinching. "We've got too much at stake not to."

Dave Nelson, the young entrepreneur did not seem as certain as the wealthiest man in America. "Mr. President, what type of attack are we talking about here?"

The President stood and walked over to the window, peering through the crack in the curtain. "If we really want to terrify the American people, it has got to be done in a public place and it has to be on film. It will be hard to top the attacks on New York. You have to hand it to Bin Laden, nothing could have captured the world's attention more than what he did that day. I'm thinking that we set off a suitcase nuke at a nationally televised football game. Football is the new national pastime anyway. And we need to do it somewhere in the middle of the country so that our people know that everyone is vulnerable. It needs to happen in Dallas at a playoff game in January."

A sick feeling entered the pit of my stomach as I turned to my brother. He looked destroyed. His entire way of thinking had changed while watching this meeting. He thought that the American dream was real and he felt safe that our government would protect us at all costs.

"Will, this isn't a bad country. He is just a bad man. All of them are bad men."

My brother didn't answer. He just turned his attention back to the monitor.

Bob Blanton, the oil tycoon from Texas did not appear happy. "Look John, you know that I am a Dallas fan. Always have been and always will be. Why in the hell would we want to blow up the most beautiful new facility in the country? Hell, I'm planning on being at that game. For God's sake, pick another city."

"Fine, Chicago then. Does anyone have a problem with Chicago?"

Dave Nelson, the young entrepreneur, looked nervously around the room. "Mr. President, what do you expect the number of casualties to be?"

"Dave, we are looking at over one hundred thousand. I know that it is a big number, much larger than I would like, but we need to do something big to insure this election. Look at it this way. Would you trade one hundred thousand lives for the security of knowing that our way of life was not going to be threatened? That this world would live in peace and that we could insure the American way of life for everyone in this country. My answer is yes."

A silence fell over the room as the group realized the enormity of the topic. This was big even for them. It would be the first attack on U.S. soil perpetrated by the group and it would cause death and destruction that was unimaginable.

Bill Douglas was a trusted member of the group and had been a part of it from its inception. "Mr. President, with all due respect, I think that this is too much. I believe that we can accomplish our goal in a way that will cause less casualties. We may not get the Shock and Awe that a football game would bring, but we can get the job done."

"What do you suggest Bill?" the President asked.

"What if we set off a suitcase nuke at a nationally televised basketball game? The live audience would not be as large, but we would have television coverage and it would be shocking. The attendance would be one fifth of the football game, so we would cut casualties by eighty thousand."

"That's good thinking Bill. Is everyone on board? Speak now or forever hold your peace."

Will and I could see that the President was strong arming the group. At least half of the group looked uneasy but wouldn't dare go against the majority. The Chinese Minister and Saudi looked elated as their own interests were being served quite well. The room was silent as the President made eye contact with each member, daring them to dissent.

"It's settled then. Mr. Zahrani, we will use your contacts to develop a team. We will supply the nuke and you can find a group of zealots that are waiting to give their lives to the cause."

They spent the next ten minutes discussing the upcoming election, moving on to the next item on the agenda without blinking. Will and I did not focus on what they were saying, they had said enough already. We stretched our legs more out of nervousness than necessity as the group discussed the declining housing market. I just didn't understand how any of these men were ever able to sleep at night. There was no way to know what was real and what wasn't. My heart was racing as I paced the length of the suite.

"So let me get this straight" Will started. "They started the recession so that stock prices would tumble and ordinary Americans would sell their stocks at low prices. Then the rich people bought those same stocks at low prices. So when the stock prices go back up, the rich people now own them at the same value that ordinary people once had."

"Yes. That is the transfer of wealth that they are talking about."

"And they think that by transferring wealth, the filthy rich have more power over the common man."

"Exactly. Apparently that is the purpose of Supero" I answered.

"So they started bird flu and release flu viruses into the air?" Will asked.

"I guess so. They think that if they keep people scared, then they will be easier to control. I just can't believe that they would kill Americans to win an election."

"I know. And President Davis is behind the whole thing. You could tell that half the room didn't want to go along with it. The man is a maniac"

"He is a maniac with a lot of power."

Our conversation was interrupted when I heard the conversation change to something that I needed to hear.

CHAPTER 16

"We only have one more topic on the agenda for today. It centers around the New World Project. I briefed you all on the project last month but to give you a refresher the New World Project was developed by two men at Georgia Tech. One was a professor and the other his student. The project developed a new way of transferring people and shipments around the country. They sell the project as good for the environment because no oil based products would be used. They sell the project as good for the middle class because it could be done less expensively than we are traveling now. And they wanted the project to offer tax breaks to companies that create manufacturing jobs in the United States. The Professor presented the project to me personally and it was beyond impressive. He showed me how the project would pay for itself within two years of completion. He had a plan to sell the technology to the rest of the world which would completely erase our national debt. And last, the project showed how the reduction in emissions would reverse global warming within a few years. The technology is legitimate. This guy is the best. And that is exactly why we had him murdered."

"What about the student?" Fahim Al Zahrani asked.

"The student is wanted for the murder of Professor Michaels. We had him a few days ago but he escaped."

"This is not acceptable" al Zahrani responded.

"I agree with you Fahim. The young man must be caught and disposed of. We had to contract the work out to a private firm because we did not want anything leading back to us but we have people on it."

"We must catch him immediately" al Zahrani continued. "If this information gets into the wrong hands, Supero could be dissolved. We would lose all of our power."

"Fahim, I heard you the first time" the President replied. "We will find this little punk and we will execute him. He has already made a lot of mistakes. It is only a matter of time."

"When the kid is gone, is that everyone that needs to be taken care of?" the Saudi asked.

"No" President Davis replied. "Harold Michaels had a wife and she knows too much. As a matter of fact, my old hag of a wife had her over to the White House last week and Sue met with me about this very issue. She knows way too much. I hate to do it, but we have to get rid of her."

Bob Blanton from Texas spoke next. "Mr. President, we may well be able to destroy this project but eventually we are going to have a problem. These nature lovers are not going to stop. Eventually, we are going to have to embrace alternative fuels. I would rather embrace them and profit than ignore them and be left without a pot to piss in."

The Saudi spoke up and was angry. "These alternative fuels that you speak of will not work. Oil is the only fuel that will work. These other fuels are nonsense."

The old Texan chuckled as he replied. "Fahim you little fart, the technology is already proven. We've been putting off this crap for twenty years. It is upon us and when it gets here your oil ain't going to be worth anything."

"Neither is yours" the President chimed in. "Look, I know that eventually we are going to have to embrace some kind of alternative fuel. But Bill Douglas and his crew have done a pretty good job of working on flex fuel vehicles and that is going to pacify the tree huggers for a while. We all know that global warming is real. We just have to put off this change for as long as we can. There will be no change for as long as I'm in the White House, I can promise you that. The only way that we will ever make a change is if Supero can profit from it."

"You must find the student and kill him. And you must kill the Professor's wife" the Saudi demanded.

The President was getting irritated. "Fahim, this is the last time that I will say this. We will take care of it."

As soon as the meeting was adjourned I got on the cell phone and called Sue.

"Sue, it's Wes. The meeting is over and it's worse than we expected. I will fill you in on everything but for now, you need to find a safe place to stay for a while. They are going to come after you. I will contact you when we get back to Atlanta."

"Are you sure Wesley? They are coming after me?"

"Yes, I am sure of it. And President Davis is the leader of the group."

"Oh my word."

"Yes, it's bad. I will tell you everything when I get back, but you need to pack some things and get out of there, now!"

"I will be gone within the hour."

We disconnected our feed to the suite when all of the members departed. We ordered two large pizzas for dinner and drowned our sorrows in pizza and a two liter Coke.

"Will, we can't just hold the President hostage with this video" I said. "We have a responsibility to report this to someone."

"Who do we report it to? I mean come on Wes, it's the President of the United States."

"We figure out who. That is what we do. I am not going to sit by and watch an entire arena of basketball fans die. That is not who we are Will. We are not that selfish."

"Well I don't want to be buried right along beside you."

"Then why are you here? You put your life at risk to plant the video camera. And you know that if we get caught in this hotel, we are both going to die. So you tell me Will, why are you here if you are afraid of getting caught?"

"I'm here because my brother needs me. I'm here because you and your save the world project has you wanted for murder and now you're caught up in the biggest scandal that I have ever heard of. That's why I'm here" he shouted.

"So you're saying that my life matters more than thousands of basketball fans. And my life matters more than all of the old people and kids that may die from a more deadly strain of the flu."

"Yeah, that's pretty much what I'm saying. You can call me selfish or whatever you want, but I'm looking out for my family first. If we blow this thing wide open, there is no telling who will come after us."

"And if we don't there is no telling what this maniac will do over the next year. Just step back and think about it for a minute. He said that he is going to bomb a basketball game. He is going to intentionally kill thousands of people just to get re-elected. And you know what is disgusting about it?"

"I know what you are going to say. That it will work."

"Absolutely. It will work like a charm. The country will be on edge and they will not elect a young guy that hasn't served in the Senate for one hundred years. He will scare them into re-electing him. Because when people feel like their life is in danger, they could care less about the economy, their job, their 401K or anything else. The most important thing to them will be that they are safe."

"Which is exactly what this group of whack jobs wants."

"Correct. So yes, we could probably bribe the President and let him off if he leaves us alone. Or we can stand up for what we believe in and do the right thing."

"Standing up for what you believe in has gotten a lot of people killed."

"I don't know if life would be worth living if I didn't stand up."

"Speak for yourself. I have a family of my own."

"Yeah you do. And what kind of world do you want your daughters growing up in?"

"A world better than this one."

We made our escape just before noon the next morning. We checked out by phone and skipped the main lobby by exiting through a side door. We both breathed a sigh of relief as we pulled away from the property.

"Thank you for helping me" I said.

"I'm just glad it's over."

"At least we got what we came for."

"And then some."

"We need to meet Sue tomorrow morning. We can pay cash for a cheap motel room tonight outside of Atlanta and then we need to fill her in. Maybe between the three of us we can decide what to do next."

"Wes, I need to get home."

"You're right. You have done more than enough and you need to quit while you are ahead."

"Are you sure you understand? I don't want you to feel like I am abandoning you."

"No way do I feel like that. You need to be with your family. You helped me when I needed you. Now you need to get out of this. It may get dangerous."

"It already is."

CHAPTER 17

The drive back to Atlanta would take seven hours and it was a long seven. After leaving Orlando there is really nothing to see except for road signs and trees. North Florida and south Georgia were both very rural areas, filled with small towns and family farms. I'm sure that it is a wonderful place to live but it makes for an extremely boring drive. Boring was fine with us given the events of the past week. Will drove and let me take a nap in an attempt to allow my body to recover from the trauma that it had experienced. I had been running on adrenaline for the past week and it was catching up with me. The fatigue that was setting in was clouding my mind at a time when I needed it working at its peak. I reclined the passenger's side front seat of the Dodge Caravan and settled into a deep sleep before we left the Orlando city limits. The drive was seven hours and I felt like I could sleep for ten.

I woke up when the Caravan slowed to a crawl.

"Where are we?" I asked.

"We are about an hour south of Macon. You've been sleeping for four hours."

"What's the problem?"

"It looks like a wreck."

Every lane was inching along as we could make out several cars with blue lights about two hundred yards ahead. As we made our way closer to what we thought was the accident, we realized that it wasn't an accident at all. It was a road block. The Georgia State Patrol was pulling over every third car.

"What do we do?" Will asked in a panic stricken voice.

"Just stay cool, act normal and maybe we will get through this without getting pulled over."

"I'm worried Wes. What if they stop us?"

"Will, get control of yourself."

As the line inched forward, I could feel my own heart beating. If we came this far, risked our lives to uncover the biggest scandal in the history of the country and were caught by state troopers in rural Georgia, I was going to be furious. I determined that they were pulling over every third car from one hundred yards away. After doing a little quick math, I then surmised that we were going to make it. The trooper directing traffic motioned for the car in front of us to pull over. We inched forward, praying to be allowed to pass. The trooper made eye contact with Will and when his finger pointed to the side of the interstate, my heart sank.

"Oh no Wes, he is telling us to pull over. What should I do?"

"Pull over and whatever you do, don't act nervous."

"Oh yeah, that's easy for you to say."

We waited for a couple of minutes while the vehicles in front of us were checked. As the trooper approached our car, I tried breathing deeply to stay calm. Will rolled down the window as the officer approached.

"Hello officer."

"License and registration please."

"This is a rental. Here is my license and here is a copy of the rental agreement."

"Where are you guys headed today?"

"I'm dropping my brother off in Atlanta then I am headed home to Kentucky."

"Just one moment and you can be on your way."

Will rolled the window up while we waited for the trooper to run Will's driver's license through the database.

"You don't have any outstanding tickets do you?" I asked.

"You know me Wes, I never get tickets."

Seconds seemed like hours and adrenaline was pumping so heavily through my body that my hands were shaking. I kept telling myself just to remain calm and we would be on our way. The trooper working with us was in his car for several minutes but we didn't start worrying until he called another trooper over. The second trooper addressed our officer then glanced back at us.

"What's he doing?" Will asked. "I don't like that look."

"Stay calm buddy. It could be anything."

I was dying on the inside. These routine road blocks were not designed to last long unless there was a problem. The troopers were deep in discussion as we waited patiently. My mind was racing, trying to determine if we should run or not. The caravan was designed for family vacations, not high speed chases. But what was our other option? We couldn't just allow them to take us here. To do so would be the end of me. We had the taped meeting with us but would anyone even listen to a wanted murderer? The wait was excruciating. Cars were passing us regularly. I saw the trooper directing traffic let six cars in a row go by. I was not feeling good at all about the situation.

Our trooper opened his door and continued talking to the second trooper. They were deep in conversation and even appeared to be arguing. There was nothing that we could do except sit and wait.

"What are we going to do if they figure out it's you?"

"We can talk right now Will, but do it very calmly. If you get animated, they may get suspicious. We have the disk. That is my savior. If they figure us out, I guess that I will just go with them."

"They may get me too. I am harboring a fugitive."

A third trooper joined the other two at the car.

"This isn't looking good" Will said.

"I know. Just take deep breaths and try to stay calm."

"What if I just took off right now? It would take them a while to react."

"I already thought of that. We are in a Caravan for God's sake. A really good ten speed could out run us. Plus they have your license brain surgeon. You don't need a wrap sheet too."

"You don't have to get smart with me. You got me into this in the first place."

"I know, I know. And I'm sorry for getting smart with you. What do you want for dinner?"

"What the hell did you just say?"

"You heard me. I'm hungry."

"You're as crazy as the President. You're wanted for murder Wes. You stupid idiot. The cops are sitting right there in front of us. They have my license and you're talking about dinner. What is your problem?"

"I'm obviously trying to change the subject to calm you down but you are so uptight that it isn't working."

"This is just like when we were little. Something serious is happening and you are joking about it. And you're picking on me. Things never change."

"Will, give me a break. We are in a very bad situation here. I get that. But freaking out is not going to help us. Are we screwed? Yeah we probably are. But there is not a thing that we can do about it. What do you think they serve for dinner in jail in south Georgia?"

Will didn't respond.

"Do you think that Aunt Bee makes dinner and brings it over? Do you think that Andy and Barney sit around singing songs for all of the inmates? Will Otis come in drunk late at night and climb in bed with us?"

"Shut up. Just shut your mouth."

The third trooper appeared to be the boss and was directing the other two. He glanced back at us once and pointed. We were caught and there was nothing that we could do. We were parked next to an open field so if I ran I would not make it more than fifty yards before getting a bullet in the back. They couldn't be calling back-up because every trooper within fifty miles was at the checkpoint.

Finally, our trooper exited his vehicle and the other two troopers walked alongside him. None of the three were happy at all. As a matter of fact they all looked extremely angry. We watched every step that they took. I clutched the hand rail of my seat while eyeing the trooper, waiting for him to make his move. He approached the car as Will rolled his window down. My poor brother had lived a lifetime since we were pulled over. I felt so sorry for him. His nerves were fried and he looked like he was prepared to just stick his hands out for the cuffs to be slapped on. I on the other hand was nervous, but the events of the past week had hardened me. I was prepared for anything.

"Is there a problem officer?" Will nervously asked.

The officer looked around. "The problem is that I work for an ass."

Will was so shocked and so elated that I had to punch him in the ribs to calm him down. He looked like a kid on Halloween walking up to the first house.

"I'm sorry for the delay guys. Drive safely."

Will pulled out very slowly and deliberately. He was so nervous that he almost rear ended the patrol car in front of us.

"Pull over at the next exit. I'm driving."

"Wes, just shut your mouth. What is happening to you? You can't tell me that didn't scare you."

"It scared me to death. But I know you Will. You get nervous in tense situations. I was just trying to get us through it."

"I know you were. I'm just glad we made it through without getting caught."

"You need to get home don't you?" I said in a sympathetic voice.

"More than you know."

CHAPTER 18

Will dropped me off at a Comfort Inn in Marietta, Georgia where Sue was waiting for me. I hugged my brother good bye and thanked him for his help. It was hard to see him go because it was comforting to have someone beside you that you trusted. I did want him to get out of harm's way and I knew that the best way for him to do that was to get back to his family. I would be forever grateful to him for his assistance. Sue looked tired and worried. She felt betrayed by the President, a man that she thought was a friend. She missed her husband dearly but was not prepared to join him in the grave.

"Sue, how are you holding up?"

"I'm doing quite well Wesley. And how are you dear?"

"I'm all right. I hate that your name has been dragged into this. I feel like it is my fault."

"It's not your fault Wesley. Now sit down and fill me in on the meeting."

"First of all, President Davis is the ring leader of the group. I brought the tape to show you. Will gave me his laptop. But I want to prepare you because it is pretty brutal. John Davis is not the man that we thought he was. He is greedy and he is ruthless. He will stop at nothing to get what he wants."

"Power has ruined many men" Sue said. "The John that I knew was a good man. He was gentle, kind and very compassionate. Wesley, did I ever tell you that we dated in college?"

"No. I didn't know that."

"It was only for a short time before I met Harold. John actually introduced us. Times were so much easier back then. There was a group of about ten of us that were determined that we would change the world. The early sixties was a great time to be young. We had a bond that we thought would never be broken. He was a good man then. I guess that some people really do change. His wife Francis was part of that group. I wonder how much of this she knows?"

"Honestly, I don't think she knows anything. He spoke harshly of her to the others."

"And you believe my life is really in danger Wesley?"

"I know that it is. You're not going to believe this."

I inserted the disk into the laptop and watched as Sue viewed the entire ordeal. Throughout the two hour long meeting, her expression never changed. She sat and watched with a stoic look on her face. Her eyes didn't express anger, surprise or even disappointment. She had seen a lot in her sixty years on this earth, but certainly nothing quite as shocking as what she was watching. That was one of her most impressive qualities, she never flinched in the face of adversity. I was watching the tape for only the second time and it was hard for me although I had just seen it the day before. As the meeting ended, I turned to my friend. It was time to develop a plan.

"Pretty disgusting huh" I said.

"Wesley, we must make several copies of this tape immediately. We need to place them in several different secure locations. That will be our bargaining chip. If this information was to ever be made public, our world would change forever."

"I think that it needs to change Sue."

"We must speak with Daniel Worth as soon as possible. Harold knew him and as I told you before, he thought that Senator Worth was the only hope that we had to develop the New World Project. I believe that he is our best bet."

"He is going to be hard to get to. He is in the middle of a Presidential campaign and I'm a wanted man Sue. There will be Secret Service with him everywhere that he goes."

"I believe that I can get him to speak with us but we must act quickly. The Saudi will not leave the President alone until we are disposed of. Let's make five copies of the disk. I will hide two and you will hide two then we will keep one copy with us at all times."

"Sounds good Sue."

When I had the copies of the disk made, I snuck into Sue's garage late at night to retrieve the old pick-up truck that Will had given me. She dropped me off about half a mile from her house then returned to the Comfort Inn. I was nervous to be back at the Michael's house because the last time that I was there, I was hit over the head and kidnapped. Before entering the garage, I checked all around the area and found no one watching the home. I had to have a vehicle and this was the only way that I knew to get one. The old truck started up on the first try and I was off to my grandparent's farm in Tennessee.

I arrived at my grandparent's old farm after a three hour drive, found my favorite old dogwood tree from my childhood, dug up the New World Project disk and replaced it with a copy of the tape from the Supero meeting.

That was my first hiding place. I slept for about three hours in the truck then started the drive back to Atlanta as the sun was rising. It was a terrible feeling to be suspicious of everyone. Every glance, every wave and every passing car was someone that wanted to kill me. My beard was full now and I kept a cap pulled low wherever I went, but it didn't help my paranoia. I was a wanted man and one misstep could put me behind bars. On the drive back to Atlanta, I stopped at a rest stop just before arriving in Chattanooga, Tennessee. It was picturesque as far as rest stops went as the Tennessee River flowed lazily by. Picnic tables were spread across the grounds as several families enjoyed a break from their trip by having breakfast by the river. I casually strolled by the water before taking out a small shovel that I had borrowed from Sue's house. I carefully dug a hole and planted my second copy of the disk. I covered the hole with dirt and replaced the grass, stomping it back to its original appearance. I then paced off the location using two points that could easily be remembered.

Upon arriving back at the Comfort Inn, I learned that Sue had placed one of her disks in a safety deposit box and mailed the other to a friend in Salt Lake City. Our security blanket was now spread to four distinct locations which could possibly save our lives. Sue's friend could be trusted and was told that should anything happen to her, the friend should mail a copy of the disk to Senator Daniel Worth. My brother was given instructions to do the same by visiting our favorite dogwood tree.

"Yes, may I speak with Senator Worth please?" Sue asked.

"May I ask who is calling?" the campaign manager answered.

"My name is Sue Michaels. My husband Harold was a professor at Georgia Tech and they worked together on an auto emissions project two years ago."

"Mrs. Michaels, Senator Worth is extremely busy at the moment. May I pass your message along to him?"

Sue was quickly irritated at the young man on the other end of the phone. "No you may not. It is imperative that I speak with Senator Worth immediately. This is very important."

"I am sorry Mrs. Michaels but Senator Worth is completely booked for the foreseeable future. I can pass a message along to him but that is the best that I can do. If you like, I can send you an autographed picture of him."

"Young man, you obviously do not understand the importance of what I am asking you to do. I must speak with the Senator right away."

Now the campaign manager was getting irritated. "Mam, I am not sure that you understand me. What part of no do you not understand? The Senator is trying to become our next President. He is in the middle of a national campaign. As much as he would like to speak personally with every voter, he can not. You must understand the position that he is in."

"If the Senator would like to insure himself the Presidency, then he needs to speak with me. I have information that will swing this election immediately. It is a major issue and I can assure you that he will want to hear it. It is of the utmost importance."

"Then if you give me the information, I will pass it along."

"I most certainly will not. I would like for you to make me a promise" she demanded.

"And what is that?"

"I would like for you to promise me that you will tell the Senator that Professor Harold Michaels' wife needs to meet with him immediately. I have some very disturbing information that will completely change this election. I need one hour of his time. I will travel wherever I need to go to meet with him. This can not wait and I will only speak with him."

"Wait one moment please."

Sue stewed in anger as she waited for an answer. She was not accustomed to being treated this way. She understood the situation and she also knew that thousands of people were probably begging for a moment of the Senator's time. But she had to meet with him. Her life was at stake, Wesley's life was at stake and the future of the country was in doubt. She would not take no for an answer.

The campaign manager returned to the line. "Your husband must be one important man because the Senator just asked a major Hollywood actor to wait outside of his office. I am going to connect you now."

"Daniel Worth" the Senator said.

"Hello Mr. Worth, my name is Sue Michaels."

"Hello Mrs. Michaels. I am so sorry to hear about your husband's passing. He was a real visionary. I really enjoyed the time that we spent together. How may I help you?"

"Well Senator, I don't really know where to start. Most of what I need to say to you needs to be said in private. My husband's death is not what it appears. He was working on a major environmental project before his death and we need to talk. I have information that will turn this election upside down. You will be shocked at a tape that I am going to show you. It is very urgent and I know that you are busy, but will you please give me an hour of your time?"

"Yes I will Sue. I am actually in North Carolina for the next three days. My office is in Charlotte. Can you meet me?"

"Yes, I will be there whenever you can see me, day or night."

"Let's meet at 8:00 tomorrow morning. Would that we O.K.?"

"That would be fine. Thank you very much and I will see you tomorrow morning."

As I watched Sue converse with the campaign manager, my stomach churned with an uneasiness that caused me to excuse myself. Only days before, my biggest worry was what I was going to have for dinner. The world had changed since then. Things were happening so quickly that it was difficult to stay focused on the next move. My fate was being decided by a campaign manager of a presidential election campaign. I had very little control and it petrified me.

After losing last night's pizza, I was waiting on the bed in our hotel room and rejoiced when she nodded her head that we had a meeting. We needed a good night's sleep because we had to leave around 4:00 A.M. for the meeting. As we each laid in our double bed, we discussed the events of the past week.

"Never in a million years could I have ever dreamed this up" I said.

"I have lived for over sixty years and not a day goes by when I am not surprised by something. I have never been more disappointed in someone than I am right now."

"I know that it's got to be tough for you Sue."

"I would kill John Davis if I had the chance" she proclaimed with hate in her voice.

"He deserves it, Sue. He deserves it."

CHAPTER 19

We arrived at the campaign office of Senator Daniel Worth exactly one hour before our scheduled appointment. We were both exhausted from the events of the past week but we knew that for either of us to ever have a prayer at a normal life, Senator Worth would have to assist us. It was a beautiful fall afternoon with the leaves turning and falling. Normally, the Georgia Tech football team would be my concern at this time of the year but unfortunately, the team was the farthest thing from my mind. Sue appeared as if she had aged a great deal over the past week. She lost her life partner and was now being hunted down by people much more adept at the game of cat and mouse than she was. We both knew that she could not keep this up for long. We were both looking for closure.

As we entered the Senator's campaign headquarters dozens of workers were scurrying about like the election was tomorrow. Many of them were volunteers that believed that the Senator could bring great change to the United States. He was the underdog, a young candidate taking on an incumbent President. But everyone in the office had faith that the American people were ready for a change and that Daniel Worth was the man for the job. We were directed to his campaign chairman.

"Hello Mrs. Michaels. My name is Jeffrey Owens. I spoke with you on the phone."

"You are much more pleasant in person Jeffrey. We have an 8:00 meeting with Senator Worth" Sue replied.

"I apologize Mrs. Michaels. The least favorite part of my job is doing phone interference but unfortunately I have to do it every day."

"No worries dear."

We were directed to Senator Worth's office. It was adorned with a lot of University of North Carolina paraphernalia. An autographed football was the focal point of his old oak desk. It was a game ball that he received after a victory over Clemson and it was signed by all of the members of the team from his senior year. His degree from UNC was proudly displayed behind where he sat. An American flag on a stand alone pole hung in the corner to his left and a North Carolina state flag hung on his right. Shelf after shelf of books lined the walls and pictures of his wife and kids were situated to each side of his desk. We waited in silence as he finished a conference call with reporters in the next room.

We stood as he entered. "Mrs. Michaels, it is so nice to meet you" he said.

The Senator was everything that you would expect. You could tell that he was an athlete that stayed in shape. He had a full head of light brown hair with small touches of grey that were beginning to appear. The hair color would change should he be elected the leader of the free world. His face was chiseled and his eyes were deep blue as polls were already indicating that women all over the country were intrigued by his good looks. From his introduction, it was easy to see that he had Southern charm going for him also. He was very approachable and non-threatening which would certainly play well with voters over the next year. It was easy to see why he was gaining ground in the polls.

"Senator Worth, thank you so much for seeing me."

"And I'm not sure that we have meet, Daniel Worth" he said while extending a hand to me.

"It is a pleasure Senator Worth, my name is Wes Holland."

"It is nice to meet you Wes. Please take a seat, both of you. Can I offer you something to drink, a bottled water maybe?"

"No thanks" we both replied.

"Mrs. Michaels, I know that we have some urgent business to attend to, but before we get into that, how are you holding up. It's only been what, a week or so since Harold's passing?"

"I am doing as well as can be expected. And please call me Sue."

"Sure Sue. And you two please call me Daniel. So what do we need to discuss?"

Sue shot me a nervous glance before she began to speak. "Daniel, I don't really know where to begin because we have a lot to share with you."

"Just take your time. I will make whatever time we need."

"Then let's just start from the beginning and then you will understand the complete scope of what we are going to tell you. Wes, why don't you start?"

"O.K., all that I ask is that you stay with me through the entire story and then it will all make sense to you."

"No problem."

I took a deep breath to calm my nerves. "I have spent the past three years working with Professor Michaels on a transportation project called the New

World Project. I will show you the presentation before we leave but the basic premise is that we developed a way to transport people and goods all over the country by using electric trams. The electric current would be inserted into our current roadways. We worked hand in hand with a group from Georgia Tech to develop a machine that cleanly cuts a six inch strip into the center of every lane and inserts an electric strip in the hole's place. The tram would attach to this strip much like a monorail and would be powered electronically to go wherever it needed to go. The system could easily be built without major disruptions in current traffic patterns. We felt like this system could be in place within five years. There would be no gasoline usage and no emissions. Every current vehicle could be retrofitted to work on the tram system. There would be one go live date and then all vehicles would be powered by this means."

"The cost for a family to travel would be roughly half of what it is today. And that is with both a federal and state tax factored in that would pay for the entire system within two years. After two years, the tax would generate billions in revenue for both states and the federal government to pay down our deficit and pay for programs that are hurting like social security and health care for the uninsured. We believed that this tax would also give us the option of cutting federal income taxes greatly without having to cut much needed programs. Basically, this system would take trillions out of the hands of oil companies and put it into the hands of the American people."

"The New World Project would be able to move people and products around the country much, much faster than we are traveling today. And there would be no more car crashes that kill tens of thousands of people each year. Traffic delays would be minimized because the entire system would be run by a computer. We are talking about a system that will completely change the way that the world operates."

The Senator was taking all of the information in, just listening to what I had to say.

"We will reverse the trend of global warming and within a few years, our climate will return to its normal pattern. We feel like the United States has fallen behind the curve in technological development and this system would put us right back on top. We would sell the technology to the rest of the developed world and pay off our national debt quickly. This is a game changer."

"Wow. Harold really was a brilliant man. And obviously you are also."

"It is quite a plan" I said. "Now there are obvious obstacles that would have to be overcome. There are a few more things that I need to explain. Just as tram like vehicles will be able to travel around the country at great rates of speed, so would goods. If you wanted food from a local restaurant and it was fifty miles away, they could have food to you in thirty minutes. Small packages and letters could arrive the same day if you needed them to get there. Shopping would take on a whole new meaning. And tourism would thrive because people could get places quicker and cheaper than in year's past. We are talking about top speeds of up to five hundred miles per hour on the fast lanes of an interstate."

"The system would be powered by a combination of wind, hydroelectric, solar and nuclear power. There are systems to back up the back up systems so that there are no major stoppages. The computer system is the same way. It is very intricate and unhackable. There are dozens and dozens of safeguards built into it."

"I like what I hear so far" the Senator said.

"Now here is the downside. Oil companies' stocks will plummet. Every driver in this country that makes a living delivering goods would be out of a job. So we must retrain this workforce to do the jobs that will be created. There will be millions of logistical jobs created as every retailer in every industry will have to step up shipping and delivery to thrive. Auto makers will have to start designing trams. And the airline industry will suffer because domestic flights will become a thing of the past. The United States postal service will no longer need drivers but they will need many workers to sort and ship letters and packages. So there will be a large re-training of the American workforce. There will be tens of thousand of jobs created to build the New World Project, but auto mechanics will dwindle because the only service that will be needed will be interior maintenance of the tram and servicing the electrical component on the bottom of the machine."

"It would be a game changer" the Senator said. "But this is unbelievable. We could completely end our dependence on foreign oil. The Middle East could no longer hold us hostage. So you are saying that your plan is workable?"

"It is completely workable and every detail has been resolved. The system is ready to go, I can assure you."

"Amazing."

"Professor Michaels truly believed that one major component of why our economy is struggling is because so many good manufacturing jobs have been lost to other countries. His idea would be to offer tremendous transportation savings to companies that add jobs in the United States. He felt like if we made transporting goods extremely cheap for those that manufactured in the U.S., then we would start getting good jobs back."

The Senator raised up in his seat and responded. "That is a good point and it has gone overlooked. Everyone likes to talk about home values being too high and the de-regulation in the banking industry but he was right. One major factor that isn't discussed is that a lot of American workers just aren't making what they used to. China is profiting and corporations are profiting but normal hard working Americans are not."

Sue had been quiet but decided to speak. "My husband was very concerned about all of our manufacturing jobs going overseas. He always said that we just don't make anything anymore. He said that it was great when you wanted to buy a television at Walmart, but he felt like the transfer of wealth by getting rid of so many good jobs would eventually bite us."

"And it bit us hard" the Senator said. "What about shipping companies. They would pretty much go away, correct?"

"They would have to re-create themselves. Large businesses would more than likely purchase shipping trams and transport goods themselves but individuals and small businesses would still have a need for shipping companies. It would not be cost effective to ship goods across the country piece by piece. So shipping companies would still have a place in the new system but it would be a smaller place."

"I don't know how familiar you two are with my platform, but one of my core beliefs is that our country must find a way to stop our dependence on foreign oil. If your system works, then we have our answer. This is exactly the type of system that this country needs. It is an innovation as amazing as the automobile or the computer. This project could reverse the economic recession, reverse global warming and re-secure our standing as the world's lone superpower. Wes, this is genius. Absolutely amazing."

"Senator, in all reality the system was not that difficult to develop. We basically took bits and pieces of technology that has already been developed and combined them. The real issue is that people are afraid of change. And some do not want change."

"Daniel, you do not know this, but before his death my husband hand-picked you as the person that could bring The New World Project into reality. He knew your belief system from when you two worked together several years ago. And he knew that you would see the vision of this project and the benefit that it could bring to the world. He was planning on approaching you in the near future and he felt that this plan would actually help you win the election. You have actually been a part of this plan for quite some time because the plan may be great but if the establishment does not buy into it, it is all for nothing."

"With all due respect to your husband's passing, the dream doesn't need to die with Harold. Wouldn't he want us to pursue it?" the Senator asked.

"Oh yes. He would want nothing less" Sue replied. She looked down and an awkward silence ensued. I too was silent, knowing that the rest of the story would be difficult.

Telling Daniel Worth the first part of the story was easy. Now he needed to hear the bad news. And this was the part of the story that would be hard for anyone to hear. I needed the Senator on my side and I needed him quickly.

"Now it gets dicey Senator" I said.

CHAPTER 20

I shot a nervous glance at Sue and then at Senator Worth.

"Senator, what we are about to tell you is going to change everything." The Senator's hopeful demeanor changed as he could see the looks of despair written all over our faces. He knew that the story was about to take a turn for the worse.

"You know when we started this conversation and I said that you need to hear me out?"

"Yes" the Senator nervously replied.

"Well now is when you need to hear me out. I am wanted for the murder of Harold Michaels."

The sentence shot through the Senator's heart like a cannon. He became nervous and fidgety in his chair as my words hung in the air like a cloud slowly drifting by.

"I did not commit the murder. He was my mentor and closest friend. Never in a million years would I harm Harold. About ten days ago, I was asleep in my dorm when some kids came home from a party and woke me up. I went to the bathroom down the hall and then three commando looking guys burst into my room. I have been on the run ever since. I learned later that night that Professor Michaels had been murdered and that I was wanted for his murder. Several days went by and I ended up sneaking over to Sue's house to tell her that I didn't do it. I had no idea who was after me but I knew that it had something to do with The New World Project. There was nothing else that it could be about."

"Go on" the Senator said. The initial shock was wearing off and he smelled a conspiracy.

"Sue believed me immediately and she also knew that there was no way that I could have murdered her husband so we began the process of trying to find out who was behind the murder."

"Did anyone know about the project?"

"Yes, unfortunately someone did."

Sue and I once again exchanged nervous glances.

"It's O.K.", the Senator said. "Just tell the truth."

Sue interjected. "John Davis was Harold's college room-mate."

"As in my running mate John Davis? As in President John Davis?"

"Yes" Sue answered.

"I was kidnapped at Sue's house. I was taken to Alcatraz of all places and beaten severely. I still didn't know who was after me. Luckily for me, I had a one second chance and was able to take a gun from one of my captors. I then turned the tables on them and they told me that they did not know who they were working for but that there would be a secret meeting in Orlando and that the group behind my abduction would be present."

"Wait. Let's step back here for a second" the Senator requested. "If I am putting this story together right in my head, you are inferring that the President had Professor Michaels murdered. And that the President came after you Wes. Am I right?"

"You are exactly right."

"Listen, we have to be very careful here. We are walking in some very dangerous territory. To ever infer that our President ordered something of this magnitude is dangerous both for you and my campaign."

"We don't have to infer it Senator" Sue said. "We have proof."

"What kind of proof?"

"Turn on your laptop and watch this" I said.

The Senator immediately pressed the intercom button on his phone. "Jeffrey, cancel all of my afternoon appointments and do not under any circumstances allow anyone to enter my office."

"But Senator, I can't do that. You have a full afternoon."

"Jeffrey, just do it."

I pulled the disk out of my jacket pocket and handed it to the nervous Senator.

"I don't know if I want to see this."

"You don't. Trust me" I said. "But you have to."

The Senator did just as I had done when I watched the Supero meeting. He took out a notepad. He pulled his chair over to our side of the table so that we all could watch the video together.

"Have you ever heard of Supero?" I asked while he was preparing.

"I have heard rumors of a secret society of wealthy people called Supero but I never knew it to be true."

"Just watch."

"Where is this?" he asked.

"It is in the downtown Hyatt in Orlando. I had three microscopic and undetectable cameras planted to tape the meeting."

The Senator pressed play and the meeting began. I watched the Senator as much as I watched the tape. He could not believe what he was viewing. For the first few minutes I would describe his expression as shocked then angry when the terrorist threat on our own people was discussed. By the end of the tape, he was simply confused. When the tape ended, he simply sat staring at his blank computer screen. The room was silent as we waited for his response. After about a minute, he closed the laptop and leaned back in his rolling chair.

"If you were to come into this office and tell me the story, I never would have believed you. If I didn't see it with my own eyes, I would not believe it. I need some time to think. I don't know what to do with this. If this goes public, democracy as we know it will be in jeopardy. We could have riots in the streets. Let me correct that, we would have riots in the streets. Can you imagine telling someone that had a loved one die of the flu that we might have caused it? And can you imagine telling the American people that their leader plotted to kill thousands of Americans and at a sporting event no less?"

"The key Senator is that it was their leader, but not their government" I said.

"Sure it was. But imagine trying to convince the American public of that. Our public doesn't trust their leaders as it is. This is like throwing gasoline on a fire."

Sue was visibly upset. Her face turned dark red and she fought back tears as her hands trembled from the rage that filled her body. "I will not allow this man to go unpunished. Not just the President but the entire group. They killed my husband and they will be brought to justice."

"Sue, I understand. Believe me I do. And I have a responsibility to the American people as an elected leader to make sure that they are punished. But I must be very careful in going about this. If we do it wrong, we could have a revolt on our hands unlike any that we have ever seen. I'm talking about things like burning down the White House. You know that we can't let something like that happen. So we need to be very careful. I need some time to think through this methodically."

"I completely understand where you are coming from Senator. But you need to understand that I am wanted by our country's law enforcement. On top of that, I have mercenaries that Supero has hired that are after me. You need to do this right, but I have to stay on the run until then. Is there anything that you can do for me in the meantime?"

"I don't want to sound cruel here Wes because I do sympathize with you, but I can't help you until officials see this tape. I just need a little time."

"I am just ready for this to be over. And I'm tired of running. I'm tired of being scared. I didn't do anything wrong. Look, I have dedicated the last three years to a project that will make the world a better place. And look what I have to show for it. Nothing."

I was growing more and more frustrated. One of the highest ranking political figures in the free world knew that I was innocent and still couldn't help me.

"Is there somewhere that you both can hide until I sort this out?"

"Yes. I know of a place" Sue said. "Let's go Wesley. We have done what we can do and Senator Worth will help us. I understand the sensitive nature of this Senator. And I apologize for what I said earlier. I need to let you do your job. It is a huge responsibility and I do not envy your position."

"The other side will claim that I am doing this to get elected. It will be politics as usual."

"The tape tells the story Senator. There is nothing else that needs to be said."

"Wes, I just don't know if we can go public with this. To do so would set our country back fifty years."

"But you can't just sit back and watch this man's reign of terror either."

"You're right. I have to put a stop to this but I have to do it the right way, with friends from both sides of the aisle. And I know that we have to move quickly. I mean my God, we can't let a horrible strain of the flu be released into the air. That is terrorism. And we certainly can not allow plans to even begin for a nuclear bombing. I can't even believe that those words are coming out of my mouth. This is catastrophic for the country, regardless of how we handle it. It is unfathomable and inexcusable. This man is insane. Not to mention the others. I have met Dave Nelson several times. Jeff Bates and I serve on the board of a charity together. And Walter Phelps has given me financial advice in the past. This is just hard for me to put my arms around."

"It's greed Senator. Plain and simple. These people really believe that if they control the wealth of everyone in the world, it will be a better place."

"It is disgusting" the Senator replied. "I have never seen or heard of something so sick in my life. But do you know the most unfortunate part of it all?" he asked.

"What is that?"

"Let's say that we clean up this mess and the public learns the truth. What happens the next time the stock market tanks? What happens the next time that we have a deadly flu season? Or God forbid, what happens the next time that terrorists hit our country?"

"The people will think that their government is behind it" I replied.

"Not just the conspiracy theorists. Every day hard working people will think that their country is trying to destroy them. Everything has changed" the Senator said as he stared blankly out his window at nothing. "It will be devastating."

"Daniel, you are the only man that I know that can rally this country around him and make the people trust us again. You are the man for the job. It will be the most difficult thing that you have ever done, but you know that it is your duty" Sue said. "You will inherit the most hostile public that any President has ever encountered. It will test you to beyond what you thought you could ever endure. But you can do it. I know that you can."

"God be with me" he answered.

CHAPTER 21

A knock on the door startled us all as we were so deep into the conversation that we forgot where we were. Senator Worth made his way to the door, fully prepared to jump down the throat of his campaign manager for disturbing him during such an important meeting.

"Jeffrey, I told you not to disturb us."

"Uh, sir, I had to."

The Senator could see on Jeffrey's face that something was wrong. He didn't see that face often.

"What is the problem?" he asked in a much more hushed tone.

"Well, the FBI is here and they are requesting to speak with Wes Holland."

"Tell them that we will be with them in a moment."

"Sir, I have been telling them that for twenty minutes. They said that I have two choices, I can either go get him or they are going to break the door down and get him themselves. They have sharpshooters positioned outside and people are starting to gather. It won't be long before the word gets out so we need to squash this quickly."

"O.K., I will have him out in one minute."

"Hurry please."

The Senator turned to us with a very worried look on his face.

"Wes, the FBI is here to take you into custody. I have no idea how they found you, but you need to go with them and cooperate."

"What if it's not the FBI?" I asked.

"I will make sure that it is. Listen, you need to give me a couple of days. I will insure your safety. You just need to trust me. Wes, you can trust me. I know that is a lot to ask after everything that you have been through but you need to, OK?"

I closed my eyes for a moment. I knew that I couldn't run forever. I was no expert at evading people that were trying to capture me. Once again, I was losing all control over my situation.

"Please just do whatever you can to make sure that no one kills me."

Just as I finished my sentence, the Senator's office doors opened and six agents burst in with guns drawn. I threw my hands into the air in an effort to show them that I would not put up a fight. The first two agents through the door bull rushed me and threw me to the ground, wrestling my hands behind my back.

"Easy!" Daniel Worth demanded. "You don't have to be so rough."

"I'm claustrophobic; could you please put my hands in front of me?" I asked.

"You should have thought of that before you decided to make us chase you all over the country."

"Identification please" the Senator asked.

"We are FBI" the lead agent in charge explained.

"I need to see some identification."

As the Senator examined the credentials, I looked at him for a response. When he nodded yes, I knew that I was in the custody of the federal government. I thought that was a good thing, but I wasn't truly sure of anything anymore. The agents grabbed my arm and pulled me up to my feet as the Senator cornered the lead agent in charge of the operation. The Senator spoke to him in a very demanding tone as I was escorted out of the building.

"If anyone harms this young man, so help me God you will never work for the FBI another day in your life."

"Sir, this young man is wanted for murder."

"I understand that you have a job to do, but I want you to listen to me very carefully. If any harm comes to this young man, I will hold you personally responsible. Have I made myself clear?"

"Yes sir."

"Where will you be detaining him?"

"We are taking him to the Atlanta Federal Penitentiary."

"You give my message to whoever you hand him off to. I mean it. No one is to touch one hair on his head."

"Yes sir."

Location: Rose Garden, White House, Washington, D.C.

"I have broken protocol because of a particularly sticky situation that has arisen. I have someone working on the inside of Daniel Worth's campaign. The two New World Project targets were spotted meeting with Senator Worth this morning. We contacted the FBI and they apprehended the kid immediately."

The President of the United States was pacing as he spoke.

"This is not acceptable" Fahim Al Zahrani replied. "You insured me that this matter would be taken care of. You and your tactics will no longer be tolerated. This New World Project will destroy my country and it will destroy Supero. You must fix this before it is made public."

President Davis was a master at dealing with foreign dignitaries during stressful situations but his patience was growing thin.

"You need to calm down Fahim. I have all options on the table now. I am not going to allow The New World Project to go public. That is all that you should care about. How I take care of it is my business."

"You were to kill the boy and kill the Professor's wife. You have done neither and now we must kill your Senator. You are making this very difficult Mr. President."

"You don't have to tell me what I already know Fahim. I am getting tired of your complaining."

"It is plain and simple Mr. President. You and your soft tactics are going to ruin everything that we have built. Shall I send in my specialty forces to do the job?"

"Give me some time and I will take care of it."

"We are out of time Mr. President. You either take care of the matter now or I will take care of it myself."

"You will do no such thing. This is my country and I will take care of the matter myself."

"Talk is cheap. It is time for action."

"Your father never would have spoken to me in the manner that you are speaking."

"My father is no longer in charge. I am in charge."

As President Davis hung up the phone, he strolled around the rose garden. Assassinating his running mate would be no easy task. He could make civilians disappear without a trace leading back to the Oval Office but his running mate was another story. The killer would need to have a motive and it would have to be done in a way that could never lead back to the Oval Office. Every layer added another person that could turn on him but he needed as many layers as possible to deflect the blame. He considered bringing Senator Worth into the secret society but it was much too risky. He was certain that the man had more information than he needed. And the only answer was to dispose of him.

Chapter 22

When the door locked behind me I realized that there was a possibility that I would never be free again. I was being held in solitary confinement at the Atlanta Federal Penitentiary. Some of the world's most notorious criminals had been housed there. John Gotti and Al Capone were probably the most famous. And now I was among them. I could hear other inmates but I couldn't see them. I was actually very relieved to have my own cell. I was a decent enough athlete, but I was by no means a trained fighter. I had no desire to have to defend myself and I surely did not want to have a boyfriend. I would fight if I had to, but I prayed that it wouldn't come to that.

My cell was twelve by twelve. I had a very small thick glass window that overlooked the recreational yard and the skyline of Atlanta was in the background. At least I could view free America in the distance. I also had a small window that looked out into the prison. My cot was small and uncomfortable but they did give me a pillow and a blanket. There was a Bible in my room and I was told that I would be given an opportunity to read books. I was also allowed to write and draw. For two hours each day, I would be given an opportunity to leave my cell and stroll around the center area of my cell block. For one hour each day, I would be allowed to roam around the outside yard. But the other twenty one hours would be spent in my cell.

The old saying that you don't know what you've got until its gone is so true. Being in prison has brought so many things to the forefront that I used to take for granted. I never thought twice about getting something out of the refrigerator, going for a walk around the block or even watching television. When those simple pleasures of everyday life are taken away, you feel them. A cold beverage is something that you relish. The smell of outside air is so much more pleasant. And the television becomes a true source of entertainment rather than something that just passes the time. When life's simple little treasures are taken away, you long for them. You want to do anything that you possibly can to bring them back. You regret taking them for granted and promise yourself that if you ever get them back, you will enjoy every moment.

I was in a truly awkward situation. I was granted a lawyer to help me with my case but I knew that I should not tell him everything that would exonerate me. I stuck to the facts of the night of Professor Michael's murder. It was odd having a lawyer that I was withholding information from that could set me free. But my patriotism and respect for our country made me keep my mouth shut. The lawyer would never have believed me anyway. I was just biding my time and hoping that Senator Worth was figuring out a plan. My freedom was in his hands.

I didn't leave the comfort of my cell until day four of my incarceration. I was so completely bored that I finally decided to take the risk and see what free time was all about. As I slowly strolled through the center of the cell block, every eye turned to me. Most of my fellow inmates were older. I decided that I was in a white collar crime cell block because most of the prisoners did not look threatening. I nodded at a guard as I passed by him and made my way to a seat in front of the television. I kept to myself because I was not looking to make new friends. The inmates didn't look menacing but they were not friendly either. They had their routines and clicks and it appeared that they wanted to keep it that way.

"You must have some pretty important friends kid" a guard said behind me while scaring the life out of me.

"Why do you say that?" I asked.

"Because we are under strict orders to watch you closely. If anything happens to you, I lose my job."

"Well I promise you that I won't be any trouble."

"It's odd getting a mandate like that for someone that has been charged with first degree murder."

"I hope that the truth comes out some day. I didn't do it."

"Yeah. Everybody's innocent in this place."

"I guess you get that a lot."

"Every day. Every single day."

The guard was a large African American man. He weighed about two hundred fifty pounds without an ounce of fat on him. I learned that he played college football at LSU and took a job in the federal prison system for the pension that he would receive after fulfilling his service. He was friendly and seemed to enjoy working in a wing of the prison that had very little violence. His name was Warren.

Warren was actually very open and willing to talk. We spent thirty minutes talking about college football. Being the Georgia Tech loyalist that I am, I went on about how Paul Johnson was the perfect coach for a school like Georgia Tech. Then we got into a friendly argument about SEC vs. ACC football. Warren was a SEC guy through and through and he loved telling stories about playing against the toughest schools in the country. He seemed genuinely interested in my background and what I was studying in school.

"I don't know if you did it or not kid, but you don't seem like the ordinary prisoner that we get."

"One day I'm taking classes at Georgia Tech and the next I'm running for my life. It is crazy. I thought that I would be worrying about mid-terms right now. And here I find myself looking at spending the rest of my life behind bars."

"Sometimes life just slaps you in the mouth. But you have to keep getting up."

"I'm trying."

I saw the words breaking news out of the corner of my eye while I was talking to Warren.

"Holy shit" an old prisoner said. "Turn it up."

"We have a breaking news story out of Lima, Ohio. Senator Daniel Worth has been shot. Repeat, Senator Daniel Worth has been shot. Senator Worth was speaking at a rally in Lima just minutes ago when a gunman appeared from the crowd and let off a string of bullets from what appears to be an assault rifle. We know that the Senator was hit in the chest. We are trying to get more details but as you can imagine it is chaos right now. We are going to go live to Bonnie Simpson who was covering the rally for us. Bonnie."

"As you can imagine, this scene is complete chaos. About two minutes ago, Senator Worth was addressing the crowd here in Lima, Ohio when a gunman appeared from the crowd. From where I was standing, he was in the center of the crowd, probably in the first two or three rows. He stood and then just started firing. The Secret Service detail that is here protecting Senator Worth reacted immediately and fatally wounded the gunman but it was too little too late. The Senator went down and we know that he was shot at least once in the chest. Everything happened so quickly that it will take some time to sort out the details. Senator Worth was rushed to the local hospital. We do not have any details of his condition at this time but he was not moving when they rushed him into the waiting ambulance. This is certainly a tragic day for our country.

Hundreds of supporters are visibly weeping here just trying to take in the tragedy. The best word that I can use to describe the scene is surreal."

"Bonnie, were there searches conducted before the event?"

"Yes there were. But there are so many people here, I would guess over three thousand, and obviously something was missed. The rally was being held out in the open and unfortunately, someone obviously made it through the security detail with a weapon."

"Do you know where they are taking the Senator?"

"We know that he was rushed to Lima Memorial Hospital and I will be heading straight over there as soon as we are finished with this interview."

"I know that you said the suspect is dead, but is there any idea as to who this person is?"

"It is just way too soon to have any information. Authorities are combing the area and it is total pandemonium here right now. It is just a terrible, terrible tragedy. We are being asked to move back from our current location as authorities are roping off the entire area as a crime scene. As I look around this stunned crowd, many supporters of the Senator are hysterical. The Senator has touched so many lives and stands as a beacon of hope and change for millions of Americans. I can see people weeping, praying and others are simply staring into space, unable to comprehend what has just happened here today."

"Bonnie, we will get back with you as soon as you arrive at the hospital."

I looked up at the shocked prison guard. "Warren, you know when you said that I must know some very important people?"

"Yeah" he answered without taking his eyes off of the television screen.

"That was the very important person that I knew."

"You mean the guy that was just shot."

"That's who I mean. I may be in real trouble now."

Our eyes turned back to the television screen as a reporter appeared standing in front of a hospital.

"I am here at Lima Memorial Hospital. I received an unofficial report that Senator Worth is in critical condition. It appears to be touch and go at this time. I am being told that the Senator is being airlifted to an undisclosed location. I will continue to give you updates as we get them. We are waiting for an official statement from the hospital and we will bring it to you live when it happens."

I lowered my head as the anchor people continued discussing the horrible news. Daniel Worth was the one chance that I had at freedom. He was going to save me and my project. Now he was clinging to life and more than likely, it was my fault. If I hadn't brought the information to him, he would still be on the campaign trail, trying to win over America's heart. Our time was up and we had to return to our cells but Warren promised me that he would forward anything important on to me. I told him that I was in danger and I think that he believed me. I have no idea why he trusted me but I felt like he would do his best to protect me.

CHAPTER 23

The President appeared distraught at the news of the assassination attempt on Senator Worth. He would address the nation in twenty minutes but could not ignore his ringing phone.

"Are you on a secure line?"

"Yes."

"Is he dead or not?" the Texas oil tycoon Bob Blanton asked.

"He is in critical condition but it's not looking good for him" the President replied.

"How in the hell did we screw this up? The shot was at almost point blank range. Good Lord John, how did we miss him?"

"We didn't miss him Bob, we just didn't kill him right away."

"Where is he?"

"A life flight picked him up. They are headed to a regional hospital now."

"Fahim won't stop calling."

"You tell him that I'm not speaking to him. It is being taken care of."

"John, that man needs to die today. Where are we on the kid?"

"He's in solitary in Atlanta but I can't get to him."

"You're the President of the United States. You can get to anybody. Start acting like it."

"I've got a nation to address, so if you will please excuse me, I need to prepare."

"What about the old lady?" Blanton asked while completely ignoring the President's pressing matter.

"She disappeared. We can't get a track on her."

"You had her when she was with the kid at Worth's office."

"I know that Bob. It's like the old hag disappeared."

"Get it together man."

At 8:00 P.M. eastern time, the President of the United States addressed the country from the Oval Office. His face was solemn as he spoke.

"Good evening. Earlier today, we received tragic news as there was an assassination attempt on Senator Daniel Worth, a true patriot for this country. Senator Worth is currently in critical condition and our prayers go out to he and his family. In this uncertain time, it is important that we remember the things that we hold dear in our lives. Senator Worth has served his country boldly and proudly and it is my sincere hope that he makes a full recovery. Let me assure you that he will receive the best medical attention that can possibly be given."

"Senator Worth and I are in the middle of an important race for the election of our next President. We have spent the past few months engaging in healthy debate regarding the direction of this country. At this critical time, it is very important that we put all politics aside and focus on the good Senator's health. I will be suspending my campaign until further notice. While the Senator and I may have different views politically, we are both most importantly Americans and we both stand for freedom and democracy. It is time for us to come to-gether as a nation and offer up prayers and good thoughts for our comrade in his time of need."

"At this time we do not have information as to why this tragedy occurred. You can rest assured that we will use the full capabilities of all law enforcement agencies in this investigation. We will continue to keep the American people updated on the Senator's progress. In tragic times, the will and determination of the American people always prevails. Good bless our freedom and God bless America."

When the door to my cell locked, I was once again alone. My life had changed again and I no longer felt safe in solitary confinement. I thought of Will and what he must be going through. He had to be worried and he knew that he couldn't protect me. If Sue made it out of the Senator's office un-scathed, hopefully she contacted my brother to let him know that I had been detained. Maybe it was time to confess everything to my lawyer. I could tell him where the tapes were. If the Senator was dead, I really had nothing to lose. It wasn't my fault if the American people revolted against their government. I might decide to revolt myself. I decided to wait and see if the Senator lived. If he lived, I would keep my faith in him. But if he died, I was on my own. It was a risky proposition because an assassination attempt could quiet even the bravest man.

The loneliest time in prison for me was at lights out. You didn't decide when the day was over, the warden did. I don't know if it was the darkness or just the fact that I couldn't do anything in the dark, but every night when those lights went out, a depression came over me like none other that I had ever felt.

The situation seemed hopeless as I stared up into nothing. I guess that lying in bed at night gave people time to think. It was the time when many people hashed out their problems and tried to work through the regrets that they had in life. Sometimes that time to think opened old wounds that were not yet healed. I was a daydreamer by nature and being imprisoned only made the situation worse. I spent my nights not knowing what the next day would bring. I never felt safe which only made the insomnia worse. I went from being a deep sound sleeper to someone that jolted up in bed at the tiniest creak.

It had only been a few days and the lack of sleep was killing me. As I lay in bed the night that the Senator was shot, my body needed rest but my brain would not allow it. I knew that the President would come after me. It was only a matter of time. There was no way to prepare. I didn't have a weapon and he had the full arsenal of the nation's law enforcement behind him. He was a terrible man but he was in control. And there was nothing that I could do. I was stuck in a cell, unable to escape. My mind was starting to go. It was becoming harder and harder to think rationally. So many things had happened in such a short period of time that I was starting to have a hard time putting everything together. I was at the point where I didn't really care about making the world a better place. My resolve was gone. I just wanted to live.

Location – White House – 10:30 P.M.

"Sir we lost the Senator."

"That is terrible news. I will send my deepest condolences to his family."

"Sir, that is not what I am saying. We literally lost him."

"What do you mean you lost him?"

"The Life Flight never landed at the Regional Medical Center. Mr. President, we do not know where he is."

"You don't just lose a helicopter. I don't care what it takes, you find him now."

"Sir, we are trying but it's like he vanished off of the face of the earth."

"Could the helicopter have crashed?"

"We don't think so Mr. President. We believe that the chopper went off course and landed somewhere else."

"You find me the Senator or I swear you will never take another breath."

"Yes sir. We will try our best."

"I don't want to hear that crap. Go do it."

The secret conference call of the Supero group was unprecedented. It was dangerous and careless but desperate times called for desperate measures. Each member of the group was summoned to be available at midnight. They all knew that the news couldn't be good if they were going to break protocol. Each member used the untraceable cell phone that they were issued upon acceptance into the group. This would mark the first time that the phones were ever used.

"Gentlemen" the President started. "I wanted to update you on the developments of today. As you know, we targeted Senator Worth today at a rally in Ohio. Things did not go exactly as planned and now the Senator seems to have disappeared."

"What do you mean disappeared?" Walter Phelps, the wealthy investor asked.

"I mean exactly what I just said. We can't find him. I don't know if he was scared and is seeking medical attention in a private location or what."

"Is there any way that he suspects you are behind the assassination attempt?" the oil tycoon Bob Blanton asked.

"No. There is absolutely no way that he would know that. It does leave us in a precarious situation. I have every belief that Worth does know about The New World Project. The kid and old lady visited him. We have detained the kid but the Professor's wife is also missing."

"This is very troubling" Fahim al Zahrani declared. "How long until we find the Senator?"

"We are trying everything that we know to try Fahim. It is just taking some time. If he is alive, he will surface. He has a race to run and he won't stay out of the limelight for long."

"It would be difficult to kill him now" Fahim admitted. "If your attempt failed, it would be very difficult to kill him now without raising suspicion."

"We just have to hope that he is dead" the President replied. "We are taking the kid tonight. He will be dead by the time that we wake up in the morning. That is one headache that will go away. So now we just have to kill the old lady and pray that the Senator doesn't make it."

Dave Nelson, the young entrepreneur was usually very quiet during the meetings. He felt like an outsider in the group. "Have we ever considered just taking our lumps and moving on? This is getting very sticky."

"That will not be acceptable" al Zahrani replied. "I will not tolerate that type of ignorance. You people have made mistake after mistake and you will not go back on your word to me."

"Jees, it was just an idea" Nelson replied. "Don't get your headpiece in a wad."

"What do you mean by that you spoiled American."

"Enough" the President said. "We are arguing like children. We will not give up this fight. Our entire way of life would be compromised. And if it means killing the Senator when and if he shows his face again, we will do it. We will poison him or inject him with some kind of toxin but the prick is not going to take the White House. I can promise you that."

"Hopefully he is dead. But if he isn't you better be careful Mr. President" Bill Douglas the former auto executive said. "The last thing that any of us want is to bring our group into the news."

"We will all take this group to our grave, regardless of the consequence. You must understand that" the President replied. "Supero will reign from now until the end of time. We will have bumps in the road but our society will rule the world."

"Here. Here" said Bob Blanton.

"I will adjourn this call now. We will take the kid tonight and I will fill you in on the Senator when we have more information.

Chapter 24

The team of four drove right to the front gates of the Atlanta Federal Penitentiary and up to the guard's station. They were in a black Suburban which was fairly standard for government officials. They were not armed but had heavy artillery in the vehicle. It was midnight, an odd hour to pick up a prisoner. The guard was suspicious from the moment they rolled down the window.

"My name is Agent Rickers of the United States Secret Service. We are here on orders from the President of the United States. We have been ordered to take one of your prisoners into custody immediately. The prisoner's name is Wes Holland. He is a suspect in the conspiracy to assassinate Senator Daniel Worth."

"Let me see your papers and identification" the guard replied.

Agent Rickers immediately handed the paperwork to the guard.

"We are in a hurry. Please work as quickly as you can."

The guard reviewed the papers and identification and then spoke into a microphone.

"I have a group here from the Secret Service. There have orders from the President to detain prisoner Wes Holland. All paperwork appears to be in order. Requesting permission to allow entry."

"Permission granted."

"Follow this road up to the main building. Someone there will assist you."

"Thank you kind sir. You take care of yourself this evening."

As the vehicle passed through the gate, the guard felt like something wasn't quite right. He had worked the guard station for over fifteen years and not once had someone picked up a prisoner at this late hour. As he watched the group pull away he decided to warn the guards in the building.

"Ron, the group is on the way. The papers were authentic and the I.D. was real but I didn't get a good vibe from the guy. Make sure that you check them out good before you allow them to take the prisoner into custody."

"Roger that."

I was in the first deep sleep of my incarceration when I thought I heard a voice say my name. I shot up from the cot as my heart pumped blood at an alarming rate. My eyes took a moment to adjust to the darkness as I saw a dark and imposing figure standing at my door. My first reaction was panic as I knew that the man was there to kill me. I backed up against the far wall where my cot was and then froze in fear, unable to move a muscle. The figure was huge and imposing. I had no fighting skills, no weapon and no plan to defend myself.

"Wes, let's go. It's Warren. I've got to get you out of here, now!"

"Warren, what's going on?" I asked in the voice of someone that was wide awake.

"Let's go. We don't have time to talk. They are here to get you."

That was all that I needed to hear. I sprang off of the cot and into my shoes, threw on my prison suit and was at Warren's side in a flash.

"We have to move quickly but quietly. If we wake any of the other prisoners, they will start stirring and making noise" he whispered. "Stay on my butt and move."

Warren threw three pillows that he brought with him under my covers then flashed a semi-automatic as we cautiously exited the cell door. He quietly closed the cell behind us and then we were off, like two mice searching for something to eat. We ran on our toes with our heads down to a service door. You could have heard a pin drop in the cell block as every prisoner was in the deep stages of sleep behind their metal doors. Warren had the master key in his hands and immediately opened the door when we arrived. Before we entered the hallway, I took one last glance at the cell block and saw exactly what I had been dreading, two flashlights and a team of men dressed in suits.

"They're here, go!" I pleaded.

We made our way down three flights of stairs, through two more locked doors then found ourselves on the ground floor of the prison. Warren led us through a maze as we ran through the gym that led to a hallway. We hustled past the medical clinic and through the open chapel before ending at another locked door. Warren fumbled with his keys as we were both out of breathe and panicked, knowing that the mercenaries could not be far behind.

The lead secret service agent had bullied his way through the red tape that was normally required for prisoner movement. He had the authority of the President of the United States which took precedence over any policy that could potentially stand in his way. He was ordered to take the prisoner immediately as it was a national security issue. He had the authority to use any means necessary to extract the prisoner including force. That was when the assistant warden relented and allowed the Secret Service team to do their job.

There was no quiet entry when the third shift guards escorted the agents to Wes Holland's cell. They were going to take their prisoner and they did not care if someone's sleep was interrupted. The team was experienced in posing as Secret Service agents and knew that the more aggressive and authoritative that they were, the less static that they would receive from whoever they were trying to fool. With help from the President, their credentials were authentic and that got them wherever they needed to go. Tonight was going to be especially rewarding. The punk kid that they tried to kidnap in his dorm room had no where to hide tonight. It was payback time and they were under orders to kill Wes Holland. Because he had eluded them and made them look incompetent before, he was going to die slowly. All four members of the group had Special Forces training and it was very rare for them to have a mission that didn't go as planned. They were embarrassed that such an inexperienced target had eluded them on a college campus and tonight was their chance at redemption. If they completed the mission all would be forgiven.

The cell block was stirring as the group of two guards and four agents marched down the corridor to Wes Holland's cell. Prisoners jumped out of bed to see what all of the commotion was about. It was very rare in this solitary block to hear so many footsteps in the middle of the night. If it happened, they knew that something bad was going on. The biggest fear was that one of their fellow inmates had hung himself. Eyes were peering through the small holes in each metal door as the group walked in unison to their destination.

"Open the cell" the lead agent demanded.

The agents did not expect a fight and wanted to respect the staff by not carrying weapons. They knew that they were dealing with an inexperienced kid and would not need weapons. A simple pair of handcuffs and the guard's baton would easily succumb their victim.

The guard found the key and opened Wes's cell door. The lights were turned on by a second guard as the team made their way into the metal box.

"What in the hell is going on here?" the lead agent asked.

The guards were waiting outside of the cell as they allowed the agents to do their work.

"What do you mean?" a guard asked as he entered the cell.

"Oh my goodness. He's gone."

The agents stood and fumed for a moment before springing to action.

"Is there anyone that could have tipped him off?" the agent asked.

"No. You just got here and all cells are locked."

"Then where in the hell is he?"

"I don't know." The guard barked into his microphone. "Sound the alarm. We have an escapee. Lock down the building. Let's search the grounds. He couldn't have gotten far. White male, early twenties. Violent offender."

Warren finally got the key into the keyhole and unlocked the door. We pushed through the darkened mess hall. I took every step that Warren took, being careful not to knock over anything that would bring attention. We scurried through the stock room, Warren unlocked one more door and then we were breathing the cold fresh air of Atlanta on a fall night. Warren did not hesitate as we sprinted to a car that was parked less than fifteen feet from the door. He opened the unlocked trunk and I jumped in before he instructed me to. I scooted to the very back of the trunk and he covered my body with blankets and sporting equipment.

Claustrophobia struck me hard when I heard the trunk door slam. I was covered with layers of blankets, it was hard to breathe and I was trapped in a small box with no way to exit unless someone let me out. I wanted to scream so badly but I knew that doing so would put me back where the bad guys were. I tried deep breathing exercises and when that didn't work I pushed some of the blankets far enough off of me to be able to move just a little bit.

Warren didn't waste a second as he kicked the car into drive and went. He did not observe the prison speed limits but he was a guard after all. We rounded the curve that took us away from the main building and headed straight for the guard shack. For what felt like the one hundredth time in the past two weeks, I was in the middle of more action than I would ever want to be in. I laid in the back of the trunk and prayed that we would make it to the open road. Warren slowed a bit on the straight two lane road that led to freedom. He did not want to look suspicious to the guard at the station. We slowed as he pulled up.

"Big Jim, what's happening man?" Warren said in his friendliest voice.

"How are you getting off so early Warren? You lucky piece of crap."

"Well Big Jim, my wife is in labor with our second kid, so I'm getting my big old butt to the hospital. She would kill me if I missed it."

"Congratulations big man. Do you know what it is?"

"We don't. Hey listen, her contractions are already pretty close together so I'm going to run. You have a good night."

The alarm sounded just as Warren finished the last sentence. He looked at Big Jim and the old guard looked right back with his eyes as big as saucers. The escape alarm had not sounded in so long that he almost forgot what it was like. "You know I've got to ask you to stay Warren."

"Big Jim, come on man, I'm about to be a daddy. My wife ain't one of those women that forgives man. She's going to have my ass for this."

I heard every word that was being said as I laid in silence not even giving myself the luxury of breathing. Could Warren pull it off was the big question? Could he sweet talk the guard into letting him leave with the alarm sounding in the background? I kind of doubted it.

"Warren, you know I can't let you go. They will have my job and I'm five years from retirement. I can't risk my career to let you go watch your baby be born. You've got to understand where I'm coming from. Just turn it around. Maybe it's a false alarm. I'll tell you what I'll do. I'm going to call the main building and see if I can let you go."

"Gee thanks, Jim. You know those by the book jerks ain't going to let me go. Come on dude. I've got to get out of here."

Warren was pleading with the old man but he wasn't getting anywhere.

"Crap. I'll make you a deal. I'm calling down to the main building and if it is a false alarm, then you were never here. You can go. But if we really have an escapee on our hands, we need you big man."

"Fine. Call them."

As soon as the old guard turned to make the call, Warren pushed the gas pedal and busted through the wooden swinging bar that prevented his exit. He knew that was his only chance to get the kid out alive. He felt for the old man and he knew that he was going to be chased but it was his only option. After breaking down the barricade, he sped into the night and the secondary plan that he had hoped he wouldn't have to resort to was now in play.

CHAPTER 25

"Prisoner is most likely in a navy Buick Lasabre heading northbound off of the premises. Repeat, escapee is most likely heading northbound off of the premises."

The lead agent screamed at the guards as they searched the first floor of the prison. "You get me to my car now!"

The team of two guards and four agents sprinted through an open door and ran around the main building to where the Suburban was parked. By the time that they arrived to their vehicle, their target was long gone. Wes Holland had eluded them again. They did not wait around for any information from the prison. Their target was gone. That was all that mattered.

President John Davis was waiting by the phone when it rang at 1:00 A.M. He was finally expecting good news in a day that had not gone as planned.

"Sir, the target vanished. He's gone."

"What do you mean he's gone."

"We did not complete the mission sir. My deepest regrets."

"Where in the hell is he?"

"Somewhere in the city of Atlanta sir. Law enforcement is searching for the vehicle."

"Back off. You're off the mission."

"Affirmative sir."

"Oh shut up."

The President was fuming. The kid had to have someone on the inside to tip him off. How else could a college kid escape from solitary confinement in a maximum security federal prison? There was no way that he was sleeping tonight so he turned his attention to who might be betraying him.

As soon as Warren floored the gas pedal at the guard station, we were on the run again. The trunk was a very uncomfortable ride as there was no seat to cushion the blows of every bump in the road. He was traveling at a very high rate of speed as we zigged and zagged our way through the streets south of Atlanta. I knew that we were going to be chased and I assumed that an All Points Bulletin had already been issued for Warren's car. The adrenaline of escaping made my claustrophobic thoughts go away. I had no idea why this man came and got me but he had certainly saved my life. There were no warnings when he rounded a curve. I felt the car want to tip at every turn but he yanked the steering wheel just in time as we flew through the streets of the city. I covered my body with blankets for some insulation just in case we crashed. If we did crash, I could be clinging to life and no one would find me.

After about five minutes of dare devil driving, the car came to a screeching halt. The engine stopped and I heard Warren open and slam his door. Within seconds the trunk was open and he was fishing through the debris trying to find me. I helped him by throwing as much as I could to the side and he yanked me out of the trunk with a very powerful arm. We were in the hood of South

Atlanta, surrounded by housing projects and seedy residents, out for a stroll at 1:00 in the morning. After glancing around, I quickly looked at Warren for guidance.

"Quick, we need to get in this van" he ordered.

I didn't respond or hesitate. I was following his lead. I jumped into the passenger's side front seat of a huge Ford Econoline passenger van. Warren pulled his Lesabre into the only vacant parking spot in the project parking lot, covered it with a tarp and jumped into the van. He had the van running and into gear before I had a chance to catch my breath. Within two minutes we were heading north on the Interstate. He had obviously planned the getaway. We drove for ten miles through downtown Atlanta and into Buckhead before a word was spoken.

"Thanks Warren" I said. "But why, why did you do it?"

"I had an old friend ask a favor and I followed through with it."

"Someone asked you to look after me?"

"Not just someone. One of the only true friends that I have ever had."

"May I ask who?"

"Who do you think?"

"Daniel Worth."

"You got it buddy."

"So you were watching me that whole time. And you knew tonight that those guys were coming to kill me didn't you?"

"Yep. Daniel told me that they would come. And damned if they didn't. They didn't waste any time did they?"

"I can't even keep my days straight any more."

"You're a lucky man, Wes. Really lucky. There is no way that you would have lived through tonight if I didn't get you out of there."

"I've been lucky a lot lately."

"I hear that."

"So where are we going?"

"I could tell you but I would have to kill you."

"Huh?"

Warren started laughing hysterically. "I guess that ain't too funny to you is it? Since you've been so close to dying and all."

"No Warren, it isn't too funny."

"Man, you've got to learn to laugh. It's either laugh or cry so you might as well laugh."

"Maybe someday."

"So where are we going?"

"I'm taking you to Daniel. He's got a cabin in the Smoky Mountains, near Gatlinburg."

"Whoa, whoa, whoa. Back up a minute. You are taking me to Senator Worth, the guy that was just shot."

"The one and only."

"Warren, talk to me here big man. Something just doesn't add up."

"He's no dummy Wes. After he saw those tapes, he started wearing a bullet proof vest. He did get shot and it hurt like hell, but he is just fine."

"Does anybody know this?"

"Just you, me and his family."

"How did he get away?" I asked

"You're going to have to ask him that. He didn't talk much when he called me today. He just let me know that he is going to be fine. And he also told me to stick around the prison tonight because he thought that those dudes were going to come after you."

"So he got shot, which obviously didn't surprise him much, then he had some kind of exit plan just in case it happened."

"Yeah, I guess. Like I said, he's no dummy. As a matter of fact he is the smartest person that I have ever met. He is always two or three moves ahead of everybody else. I guess that's why he is running for President."

"I guess so. Wow. I am a lucky man."

"You ain't no man. You're still a kid."

"Warren, I may not be a man, but I'm sure not a kid anymore. I don't know what you would call me."

"I call you lucky."

We drove for an hour in silence on I-75 that would take us to Chattanooga, Tennessee. From there, the interstate led right to the foothills of the Smoky Mountains. It was about a three and a half hour drive and I didn't mind a second of it. Anything beat being confined to a prison cell. I had only been locked up for a few days but it felt like years. I enjoyed the drive and even forgot that we were wanted men. It just felt good to be free. And I was so thankful that someone was looking out for me. I was beginning to think that there just might be hope for the world after all. Warren looked like he was about to doze off so I decided to break the silence.

"So how did you meet Senator Worth?"

"Well, he was linebacker Worth when I met him. He was the prettiest linebacker in the NFL."

"So you and he both played in the NFL?"

"We both had a cup of coffee. I was a defensive end and he has a middle linebacker. We played for the Chiefs back when the Chiefs were good."

"That is so cool."

"I guess. Daniel and I roomed together on the road. Neither one of us got to play much but that man saved my life."

"Really. How's that?"

"It's kind of hard to talk about Wes. When you're trying to get playing time and you know that you're close to getting cut, sometimes you do stupid things to try to get ahead. I started doing steroids. Daniel was always jumping down my throat about it but them things made me as strong as an ox."

"So they worked then?" I asked.

"Oh yeah, they worked. The problem was that they worked too good. I thought that I was invincible. One night I got in a bar fight and took on six or seven dudes. They beat the crap out of me. They broke my nose, I still have a lump in it. And they cracked a few ribs. But the worst part was that one of them broke my arm. I tried to rehab as fast as I could so that they wouldn't cut me. And then I got hooked on painkillers. It got bad Wes. They were frying my brain. The Chiefs cut me and they cut Daniel not long after that. I got real depressed and tried to kill myself. And that's when he came and got me. He moved me into his apartment while he was attending law school at Vanderbilt and he took care of me. I didn't have the money for rehab so he made me his project."

"He didn't have to do that did he?"

"No he didn't. But he cared for me when nobody else did. And I was an ass back then Wes. I was mixing those painkillers and steroids and I was a completely different person. I would have those steroid rages that people talk about. And that man stuck with me through the whole thing. He even took out student loans and paid for me to go to Belmont University. Can you believe that? He was a young man then Wes. And he borrowed money to send me to school. That man is a saint."

"That has got to be one of the greatest stories that I have ever heard."

"I would give my life for that man. He could ask me to jump off of a building and I would do it. He made me the man that I am today. If he didn't help me, I would either be dead or a junky somewhere."

"Think about what he's doing for me. He doesn't even know me and he's helping me. I have talked to him for maybe two hours and he is doing everything that he can to help me. It is just unbelievable. And you too Warren. You risked your job and your life for me tonight. He may have saved your life but you saved mine. And I will never forget it for as long as I live."

"Daniel said that you were a good guy and I was happy to help. He said that the people that were going to come get you weren't who they said they were. And if Daniel tells me something, I take it as the gospel. I'm telling you Wes, there are not many men on this planet that are as good as he is. Salt of the earth."

"What made you go into prison work?" I asked.

"About eight years ago, Daniel helped me get the job. And I really like it. I've been in your cell block for five years and those guys don't give me a bit of trouble. Most of them are rich guys that got caught stealing money and stuff like that. Most of them are real polite and just want to do their time. It's actually a pretty easy job."

"You're going to lose it now aren't you?"

"Daniel said don't worry about it. He said that he knows a bunch of stuff that nobody else does and that everything would be fine. I trust him."

"So do I Warren."

Chapter 26

When we pulled up to the chalet in the mountains, it was almost five in the morning. We were both exhausted from the whirlwind night and a guard met us in the driveway.

"What's up Jack?" Warren said.

"Warren. It's so good to see you. How have you been?"

"I can't complain Jack. I'm tired and hungry but other than that, life is good. Meet my friend Wes."

The security guard extended a hand to me and helped us get our bags into the huge chalet. It was two stories and made entirely of pine. When you walked into the place, a huge open living area greeted you with a winding staircase on each side of the room that led to the second level. The entire home was open with lots of windows to take in the breathtaking view. A very large fireplace was the focal point of the main room with two comfortable leather couches to choose from. A chef was already awake and preparing breakfast as we entered the chalet.

"You guys will find your bedrooms up the staircase to the left. Go ahead and drop your bags in there and then we will have breakfast ready for you. After breakfast, you can catch up on some sleep."

"That sounds good to me. I love the smell of bacon" Warren declared.

"I would know that loud mouth anywhere" Senator Worth said while walking out of his bedroom on the second floor. A walkway that stretched the entire length of the second floor overlooked the main living area.

"Danny boy. How are you big fella" Warren said.

"Hello Wes. It's good to see you" the Senator said.

"And it's good to see you Senator. I'm glad to see you in one piece."

"That was a scare. I'm just glad they aimed for the chest."

"Yeah, you wouldn't know what to do if they hurt that pretty face of yours" Warren said as he laughed. "The million dollar smile. My man Danny."

"It's good to see you Warren. Now drop your bags off so you can eat me out of house and home."

"That sounds good to me."

For the first time in over ten days, I felt safe and secure. I was with a Presidential candidate and for once, we had a security detail instead of me being guarded by someone. Senator Worth had a sense of confidence about him that made me feel very comfortable. I was hoping to get something to eat and then get some good, sound sleep. I knew that a few short hours of sleep without the fear of being murdered would do wonders for my body. Warren threw his bag in his bedroom and the Senator found me some fresh clothes and we sat down for a breakfast that was fit for a king.

I believe that I gained a pants size while devouring a good southern home cooked breakfast. We had scrambled eggs with cheese, bacon, sausage, grits, hash browns and my favorite, biscuits and gravy. It was exactly what I needed, a good home cooked meal that was not served to me through a hole in the door. As the sun rose over the eastern horizon, the beautiful view became visible. We were in paradise. The chateau was built into the side of a mountain with a breathtaking view of the Smoky Mountains. A morning fog hung over each mountain top as the sun tried to peek through the haze. This was how the other half lived and I liked it. It was the Senator's escape from the everyday grind. His entire life had been devoted to others but even he needed an escape from his daily routine. As breakfast was winding down, Warren retreated to his bed while the Senator asked me to stay behind to talk.

"I can't thank you enough for what you did for me" I said. "I have been feeling very guilty ever since we met because I don't think that there would have been an attempt on your life if I didn't meet with you."

"Wes, do not think that way. I personally think that it was inevitable if I were elected President. Now that I know what I know, this group would have taken me down eventually. I feel so naïve. I have been in Washington for eight years, but I had no idea that this type of organization actually existed. And I had no idea that people would stoop to the level that this group has. I'm actually glad that we met because I knew to prepare for what might come. At least now I know what I am dealing with."

"I have been the definition of naïve through this entire ordeal. I was stupid enough to believe that if I created something that would help the world, people would just accept it and love me for it. But Professor Michaels knew better."

"Yes he did. But he still paid the ultimate price. Even he did not realize the scope of Supero."

"Have you decided what your plan is going to be?" I asked.

"I'm getting there. The plan has changed completely since they tried to kill me. The gloves are off now and I do not care about the President's legacy. I guess that I never should have. That is just another sign of my naivety. But you live and you learn. Don't you agree Wes."

"I've learned a lot over the past couple of weeks but I just haven't been sure if I was going to live to use what I learned."

The Senator laughed. "Good point. We've both had some close calls."

"If you didn't have Warren help me, I would have died last night."

"If the shooter went for my head, I would have died. We are both

lucky. But we both believe in something that is greater than ourselves and there is something to be said for that."

"So what's the plan?"

The Senator sat back and wiped his hands with his napkin, picked at his teeth with a toothpick and played with a butter knife that had gone untouched throughout breakfast.

"I am going to conduct a conference call in about an hour with ten members of Congress. They have no idea what the call is about and they do not even know that I am the person that is conducting it. They believe that I have disappeared, just like the rest of the country. But I must get back into the public eye. The reason that I asked you to stay is because I would like for you to witness the call. I know that you are exhausted, but you deserve to be a part of this."

"I would love to watch."

"Watch nothing. You are going to be a part of the call. Wes, you have been tortured by this group. Wouldn't you like to take part in taking them down?"

"Yes sir, I would. There is nothing that would please me more at this point."

"Good then, we are on in an hour. Why don't you take a shower and get cleaned up. We don't want you to look like a prisoner during your first appearance in front of Congress."

"Good point."

I was no longer tired. Senator Worth was letting me in an inner circle that civilians rarely viewed. I was going to be involved in the most controversial scandal in the history of the country.

"Daniel, can you trust the Congressmen that we are speaking with?"

"I don't know who I can trust anymore but if they don't do what I say, the world will know the truth very quickly. We hold the cards here Wes. We have the power."

The hot water cascading down on my aching body was the best medicine that I could have possibly taken. I stood in the shower and didn't move for several minutes, simply enjoying the heated pellets as the made their way from showerhead to drain. The water helped to wake me up and as the soap cleaned my filthy body, my fear and doubt disappeared. I had always been on the right side of this dilemma but now I had someone with me that mattered. I wasn't just a lonely unknown voice anymore. My team held the power and we would use it to right many wrongs. After cleansing my body, I closed my eyes and let the water continue to massage me while I reflected on the great difference that the past twenty four hours had made in my life. The one man that could save me had not only survived but he was ready for revenge. Revenge was exactly what I needed and I was more than happy to do whatever I needed to do to get it done.

I sat next to the Senator on his couch as we prepared for the call to begin. He was taking every step that he could think of to insure our safety. A backdrop was draped behind us so that no one could see our location. The call was going to be a video conference, my first. I was extremely nervous as the time approached. It was difficult to internalize the historical implications of what we were about to do. The news would be documented in history books forever. The secret society would surely be the subject of movies and books. And there was a very good chance that the country would completely revolt against its government. Obviously that was the most disturbing matter of all. But we really had no other choice. To continue to allow a madman to operate above the authority of the law to serve his own self interests was not possible.

CHAPTER 27

The look on the congressmen's faces was priceless when Daniel Worth appeared before them. They knew that they were going to be a part of a very important conference call. They knew that the call would be a matter of national security and would be highly confidential, but they had no idea that the call would be with the Presidential candidate that had been presumed dead for two days. As far as they knew, the Presidential candidate was missing, a mystery that thousands of law enforcement officials were trying to solve. So it was understandable that seeing the Senator's smiling face took them back a bit.

"How is everybody?" Worth started.

No one responded for several moments. They simply stared at the television screen, wondering what in the world the Senator had up his sleeve. The nationwide manhunt could be cancelled. He was in fact very much alive and appeared to be in good spirits. They had no idea why he had scheduled the conference call and several members of the group were uneasy about a secret meeting with a Presidential candidate.

"Is no one awake yet today? I said how is everybody?"

"The question Senator Worth is, how are you?" The question was asked by Milton Jackson. Jackson was a sixty five year old Congressman who had served the great state of Missouri for most of his working life. He was the senior member of the group that Senator Worth had called together and would act as the spokesperson.

"Well as you can see, I am indeed alive and well. I have never felt better."

"Can you please explain what happened?"

"I will tell you all what you need to know but I am going to be doing most of the talking today. I have some very troubling news to share with you today. As you know, I have called together this group so that both parties could be represented here today. The matter that I am going to share with you is very delicate in nature and will require both parties to work together if we are going to make it through this.

"My goodness Senator, is the world about to end? What can be so awful that would require you to prep us like this?" Jackson asked.

Daniel Worth ignored the question. "First of all, please let me introduce Wes Holland. Wes is a young man that was a student at Georgia Tech. He is a brilliant mind and unfortunately is also at the center of our reason for meeting this morning. Wes and his mentor at Georgia Tech developed something called The New World Project. The project lays out a plan to end our dependence on foreign oil completely within five years. It is a transportation system that uses electricity exclusively. The plan modifies our current vehicles to run on an electrical track. There are no drivers. Computers guide the vehicles wherever they are programmed to go. Goods and services use the same system. It sounds very radical but when you see the presentation, it is actually very practical. The plan uses several current energy sources to power the system. It is very ingenious and every potential pitfall is addressed."

"It sounds very space age" Congressman Jackson said. "But we will take your word for it. What's next?"

"Congressman, you might as well sit back and keep your mouth shut because this is going to take a while. Believe me, you are going to want to hear the entire story."

The Congressman did not reply as a scowl covered his face.

"As I was saying, the system was great and they had reached a point where it was time to present. Wes's professor did present the project to the President and that is where the story begins. Professor Harold Michaels was murdered. That same night, there was a kidnapping attempt on the young man sitting beside me. Wes was then made the prime suspect in his mentor's murder. The story goes on and on but the basics are, some very important people did not want this project to come to fruition. They went to great lengths to see that it didn't. This young man has been beaten, arrested and chased all over this country."

"If he is wanted for murder, shouldn't he be chased and arrested?" the annoyed Congressman asked.

Once again, Senator Worth ignored the question.

"Wes was able to extract some information from his kidnappers and he learned that the people behind the entire ordeal were to meet in Orlando. He found the hotel where the meeting was to be conducted to find out exactly who he was dealing with. And the answer is very disturbing."

The congressional panel was beginning to grow impatient.

"Excuse me Daniel, but why can't you just come out and say what you are trying to tell us?" Senator Worth's old friend, Elizabeth Brown was speaking. She was a sweetheart Congresswoman from Virginia. "Something is just not right with you. Get on with it already."

"Hi Elizabeth. You never have been very patient have you? All right. I will just come out and say it. President Davis had Harold Michaels killed.

He is trying to kill Wes Holland and he is a member of a secret society known as Supero. The group is made up of some of the wealthiest and most influential people in the world. Their mantra is to control the world by fluctuating economies to create more wealth for the elite upper class. They control the world by unleashing fear on its people. And they control the world through political policy. The group is stunningly disgusting and John Davis is their leader."

Congressman Jackson spoke up. "I have heard of some ridiculous ploys over my twenty five years in Congress, but this is the worst. You sound like a fool Senator. And I think that you faked your own assassination. You need to come out of hiding and tell us what in the hell you are doing."

"Congressman, I respect you dearly. You have dedicated your life to this country. But today, you need to listen. Do not speak, just listen. If you know anything about me, you should know that I can not stand the silly little games that are played in Washington. I come to you today with a heavy heart. The things that you are about to learn will change our country forever."

"Daniel, I don't mean to cut you off here, but do you have any evidence? You know that we need it to level any kind of accusation of this magnitude." Elizabeth Brown trusted her friend but even she was having a hard time believing what she was hearing.

"All right ladies and gentlemen, make sure that you are sitting down because I am about to show you a video that you will remember for the rest of your life."

The Senator played the video for the group. He and I watched the pained expressions on each of their faces as they viewed the horrible tape. You could watch hope disappear from each of their eyes as the damning evidence was made more and more conclusive with every sentence. By the half way point, each member was disgusted. They could not believe what the President was saying. By the end of the tape, you could see the worry in their faces as they realized that the task before them would be a great one. When the tape ended, their faces were solemn and they sat in silence, unsure as to what the next move should be.

Congressman Jackson finally spoke up. "I apologize Daniel. I had no idea."

"No apology is necessary."

"Well this tape can't go public. We would have anarchy in the streets."

"Listen, there is one more thing that I haven't told you all. I am certain that the President tried to have me killed. I was given a heads up by Wes, so I was wearing a bullet proof jacket everywhere that I went. But it was too close for comfort and now I am taking the gloves off in this campaign."

Elizabeth Brown spoke up. "Daniel, we can't make this tape available to the public. It would destroy our democracy."

"It doesn't have to be made public if you all do as I ask."

"What might that be?" Congressman Jackson asked.

"The President is to be removed from office immediately. A congressional panel can determine what will and will not be admissible in court. But this man will be held accountable for what he has done. Each member of the group will be arrested and have the book thrown at them."

"And what are we supposed to tell the American people?" Jackson asked.

"I really don't care what you tell them. You can say that he was laundering money, abusing his executive privileges. I really don't care what you say, but if you do not want that that tape shown to the American people, you will do as I say."

Elizabeth Brown looked very disturbed as she spoke to her friend. "Daniel, I hear what you are saying but this isn't like you. You come to us with these lofty demands and refuse to negotiate. What gives?"

"Look Lizzy, you know that I trust you. I would trust you with my life. But someone tried to kill me a couple of days ago and I am going to protect my health. I don't know who is good or who is bad in that room with you. So, yes I am forcing the issue. How in the world can you even begin to protect that animal? Lizzy, he is going to kill thousands of Americans at a sporting event. Come on."

"Daniel, I am not protecting him. I do think that he needs to pay dearly for abusing his power. But we do need to be very careful in what we tell the American people. We can not handle a revolt right now. The country just can not withstand it. So let's put our heads together and come up with something that we can all live with."

Chapter 28

The sniper had been scouting the area for two days. He had his position secured and his equipment was ready. The assault rifle could easily handle the three hundred yard distance from his self made tree stand to the living room of the chateau. The young prisoner had arrived before dawn just as the President had advised. The Senator had been visible in his scope several times throughout the morning. The security detail was decent but had not come close to detecting him. The former Green Beret was the best in the world at camouflaging himself in a one hundred foot tall treetop. The tree had been his home for most of the past forty eight hours. The security detail scanned the area each hour by four wheeler but they were not prepared for someone as adept at being invisible as he was. He was spotted the previous morning but it was by a passing buck. He was ready to act, he just needed the go ahead.

"Mr. President, we have Senator Worth's location. As you predicted, the boy is with him. He arrived this morning. I have a sniper in range and he is prepared to take a shot when you are ready."

"Is the Senator hurt?" the President asked.

"No sir, according to my sniper he has been very active this morning. He is showing no signs of a chest injury."

"That little weasel was wearing a vest. Listen, have the sniper take him down when he has a shot. I want a head shot this time. And I want you to hear me, we can not miss this time. We must end it now. Do you understand?"

"Yes sir."

"I will not agree to anything that includes John Davis being in the White House for one more day. He must be removed from office immediately."

"You are just trying to win an election" Congressman Jackson sarcastically remarked. "You selfish piece of crap."

"If I was just trying to win an election, I would have already taken this to the public. Everyone in this country could know exactly what happened by dinner tonight. But I didn't do that. I care about this country more than winning the election. And I have had about enough of your mouth Congressman."

"Daniel, don't listen to Congressman Jackson. Listen to me. We need some time to get this done. We can't just walk into the White House this evening and escort the President out. We need more time."

"Lizzy, I don't have more time. You do not understand. If I wasn't wearing a vest two days ago, I would be dead right now. The man is trying to kill me. Help me out here. I want to do the right thing, but it has to be done on my terms. End of story."

"How about forty eight hours. Can you give me that long?"

"No. Midnight tonight is the deadline. Either he is out of office or the world learns what John Davis is really about."

"So you are prepared to accept the blame for hundreds of thousands of rioters. Politicians may die, their families may die and you don't care. You just want to save your own butt then huh Dan." Elizabeth was visibly upset.

"What if he releases a flu virus tomorrow? What if he decides to move up the bombing date. What if he kills me tonight?"

Time stood still as the bullet left the barrel of the gun. It was a chilly but clear morning without a cloud in the sky. Birds were chirping and the squirrels were scurrying around preparing for a winter in the nest. The leaves on the trees were slowly falling, floating from the branch to their final resting place. A small stream ran beside the chateau providing the steady and relaxing sound of running water. The Senator and the boy had been still for over an hour, conversing on a computer. The wind was calm which made the job so much easier. The shot was clear, the target was stationary and the timing was perfect to end it now.

Warren jumped out of bed at the sound of the rifle firing. He knew that trouble must be brewing and he would rush to the aid of his friend. He went from a deep sleep to fight mode in less than ten seconds. He threw on his pants, grabbed his rifle and burst through the bedroom door, prepared for anything that might occur.

When I heard the shot, I immediately started feeling around on my body to see if I had been shot. Panic set in as I dove to the floor, trying to escape a barrage of gunfire that was surely to follow. I used the couch as my shield and covered my head with my hand, praying that I would not hear another shot. After ten seconds of silence, I mustered the courage to take a look around the room. My safe haven was safe no longer.

The Congressional panel jumped at the sound of gunfire through the computer. They were unaware of the Senator's location but did believe that he was in danger. They could not believe what they were hearing as the Senator fell to the floor as the sound of the shot rang out over the microphone. They each felt helpless as they watched the events unfold. They prayed that they were not witnessing an assassination. They also immediately felt guilty for second guessing their colleague and criticizing him for going into hiding. He was clearly a wanted man. Someone wanted him dead and was not going to stop until it happened. It was time to act, if it wasn't too late.

"Senator!" the lead security guard shouted as he sprinted toward his boss. The shot had startled him as it came out of nowhere. His immediate responsibility was to the Senator. He would check him first then send someone else after the gunman. He had been on the second floor, using the bathroom when the shot rang out. He took the stairs four at a time, trying to will himself to his startled boss. Two assassination attempts in forty eight hours were more than he ever hoped to endure.

"Sir, can you hear me?" he asked after diving across the hardwood floor and sliding to Daniel Worth's side beside the couch where he had been sitting. "Are you hit?"

"Security One this is Security Four, come in."

"This is Security One."

"Sir, I just shot a sniper in a tree about three hundred yards due South of the building. I believe that he was getting ready to line up a shot. He was about one hundred feet up and he fell to the ground so I think he is gone sir. I am in route as we speak. Should have confirmation in less than a minute."

The Senator heard everything that was said over the microphone as did the Congressional panel that was watching via video conference. He sat up and dusted himself off. He was visibly shaken. He tried to remain steadfast and brave during these treacherous moments but it was difficult. He was not accustomed to people trying to kill him. He did not think that he would ever get used to it.

"If you didn't believe me before, do you at least believe me now?" he asked the group.

Senator Bill Mathews from Kentucky spoke. He had been silent up to this point. "I have seen enough. Between the tape and now this, we must act on the President immediately. Senator Worth, your location is compromised so you must find a secure location quickly. I am sorry for the barrage that you received from us today. I am sure that you understand the magnitude of what we must do so it is very important that we insure that we are doing the right thing for the American people. This man is dangerous and can not be trusted. We must remove him now. Be careful Senator."

"Thank you Bill. I am going to get out of here. I will watch the news via satellite to remain informed of your progress."

"Take care of yourself Dan" Elizabeth said.

"Good luck to you all. I know that what you are about to do is not going to be easy. We will work together to make sure that it is presented in a way that allows the American people to still believe in our way of life. I will not use this as a way to attack the other party but whoever is chosen to run against me will be up against monumental odds."

John and Francis Davis were wrapping up the dinner that they were hosting in the White House when the Vice President arrived. He was joined by several members of Congress and they were waiting for the President outside of the Oval Office. He was unaccustomed to being summoned by the second in command so he knew that some type of crisis was on the horizon. He politely kissed his wife good night as he knew that he probably had a long night ahead of him.

"This can't be good" he joked while greeting the group.

Vice President Marks looked anxious. He was always calm and cool in the face of crisis, but something was certainly bothering him tonight. He was pacing the length of the Oval Office as the President escorted the group into his office.

"What is it Mr. Vice President?" he asked.

"John, we have some very bad news. You and I have known each other for over twenty years which only makes what I have to tell you that much more difficult."

The pacing stopped as the Vice President took a seat directly in front of his boss. The other members of Congress were silent and solemn as they gazed at the Commander in Chief.

"Wayne, what is your news?"

"Sir, you are going to be impeached tomorrow morning. We have video evidence of your recent meeting with the other members of Supero. Sir, you have a lot of questions to answer."

"It must be a fake" the President assured them. "What do you mean by Supero? What is that exactly?"

"John, do not insult my intelligence. We know it all. We know everything. We have seen the tape from your meeting in Orlando. So don't play these games with us. We are all very disturbed by what we saw. What you are doing is unfathomable. I feel very inadequate because I had no earthly idea that you were capable of these types of things."

The President turned his back to the group by swiveling his chair one hundred eighty degrees. The room was silent but tense. It was his move and he knew it. The day had come that he dreaded more than any other.

"The people of this great country elected me to be their leader. And that is exactly what I am doing, leading. You may not agree with my tactics or philosophies but every move that I have made is in the best interest of this country. People need to be led and they do not always know the sacrifices that are necessary to reach greatness. You may judge me and the American people may judge me but I have always acted in the best interest of this country."

"John, you will be removed from office immediately. We have made the decision tonight that the tape will never be shown to the public. The backlash that would occur is far too dangerous to even consider taking this to the people. A decision has been made to charge you with abuse of power, money laundering and conspiracy to commit murder."

"Whose murder?"

"Harold Michaels."

"The son of a bitch won in the end." The President turned to face the group. "The path that you are choosing is dangerous."

"Mr. President, the path that you have chosen has put you in the position that you are in today. You will be quietly escorted off of the premises tonight. If you cooperate fully, you will be placed under house arrest at your home in Virginia."

"And what about the other members of my group?"

"Warrants have been issued for each of their arrests. They will each be charged with the same crimes that you will be charged with. Each member of your secret society will have no contact with the outside world for a period of twenty years. You should consider yourself lucky sir."

"I will do no such thing. Our democracy is at risk. No one in this room can begin to fathom what it takes to run the world that we now live in. You will regret this day for the rest of your lives."

"That is a risk that we are willing to take sir. The guards are waiting. We will allow you to ride with your wife to your home in Virginia where you will explain the entire situation to her."

CHAPTER 29

Will Holland was watching his favorite television show when the news bulletin interrupted. The lead anchor of NBC news was on the screen. Will knew that lead anchors only returned to work when something major occurred.

"We now interrupt this broadcast for a breaking news story."

The words "Country in Crisis" appeared on the screen and Will turned the volume up on his remote control.

"Good evening ladies and gentlemen. We have interrupted your regularly scheduled program because we have just received unbelievable news from the White House. We have unofficial reports that President John Davis has been taken into federal custody and will be relieved of his duties as President of the United States immediately. Our White House correspondent is reporting that President Davis will be convicted of the following charges: money laundering, abuse of power and conspiracy to commit murder. Details of his arrest have not been confirmed by White House officials but we are told that Vice President Wayne Marks will be assuming the role of Commander in Chief effective immediately. We have a source that spoke to us on the condition of anonymity and our source is telling us that the President was involved in a plot to have a prominent Professor at Georgia Tech University murdered. The source went on to say that the President will be convicted on charges of laundering millions of dollars each month from defense contractors in Iraq. The source added that there will be additional arrests connected with the same conspiracy. The un-named persons will include several prominent United States citizens and possibly two or three international businessmen."

"The news comes at a particularly difficult time in our nation's history as unemployment rates continue to skyrocket and the stock market has remained in a state of uncertainty. We can certainly expect the markets to drop tomorrow morning with this deeply troubling news. Let us take you now to the White House where Vice President Marks is conducting a news conference with reporters."

The Vice President appeared in the White House press room. He had certainly composed himself as he appeared from a side door to address the nation.

"I will be making a brief statement this evening. I will not be taking questions. Ladies and gentlemen, effective immediately I will be assuming the role of President of the United States. Earlier this afternoon, several members of Congress and myself were briefed on a series of events that we felt would compromise John Davis's role as our President. President Davis has served this country for most of his adult life. Unfortunately, several decisions that were made during his time as our Commander in Chief do not reflect the qualities that our leader should possess. While President Davis acted on an agenda that he felt best served our country, it has been determined that his actions were not deemed appropriate and therefore he will be relieved of his duties. Let me assure you that I will act in the best interest of this country and will do so with the full cooperation and advise from our elected Congress. We will work tirelessly to boost the economy, lower unemployment rates and maintain our standing as the greatest nation in the world. Ladies and gentlemen, we will pull together as Americans have so many times during critical periods in our country's history. We will weather this storm and come out of it a stronger nation. I would like to commend President Davis for the service and dedication that he provided over the past three and a half years. I look forward to serving as your President. God bless the great people of this country and may God bless America."

I watched the speech with Daniel Worth and his entire staff. We were staying in a suite on the Penthouse floor of the downtown Hilton in Charlotte. The Senator tripled his security staff after the failed attempt on his life in Tennessee. I felt as secure as the gold in Fort Knox as armed guards manned every entrance to the floor. There was a guard positioned in front of my room and two guards were camped out in front of the Senator's suite. In addition, there were several snipers that were strategically placed on the roof of the hotel and across the street. Daniel Worth would take no more chances. He turned the television off as soon as the speech ended.

"O.K. gang, we are going to strike while the iron is hot. We have a little less than a year until election day so a big spend now goes against our budget plan but a chance like this only comes around once. The President got what he deserved and now it is time to take control of this race. I will be purchasing a thirty minute television spot on the four major networks for this coming Monday. During the thirty minutes, I will lay out my plan of action to the country. There will be a focus on the economy, jobs and The New World Project. Wes, you are going to have to help me write this speech because everything ties in together. I can sell the country on environmental change if we clearly show them how the project will create jobs and stimulate the economy. This speech will make or break the campaign. It is a big gamble but I believe that we can pull it off. The door is wide open right now and we are going to be proactive in swinging voters while they are upset with the current administration."

"The worst mistake that we can make right now is to take anything for granted. One year is a long time and we all know that one mistake can cost us the election. This speech must be flawless, we must all be preaching the same message and we must understand how to comment on the current situation."

"And how do we comment on it sir?" the campaign manager asked.

"We will keep our comments brief. We will state that it is deeply troubling that the President abused his power and used taxpayer money to line his pockets and the pockets of his colleagues. We will then state that business as usual in Washington is just not getting it done. At that point we will lay out the basics of how a Worth administration will make the country better. Are there any questions?"

No one commented.

"Good. Listen, we must remain compassionate but firm over the next few weeks. Americans are going to be angry and confused. We must be comforting to them in everything that we say. We must be confident in our answers and we must convince our citizens that our way is the only way out of this quagmire. We have a tough battle ahead, but if we work together as a team, we will prevail."

Location – Former President John Davis's residence.

"John, I am deeply troubled by the events of the past twenty four hours. The future of our society is at risk. Your actions have brought our group too close to the limelight. This is not acceptable."

There was only one voice in the entire world that intimidated John Davis. He had never met the man known only to the group as The Enforcer. He had spoken to The Enforcer when necessary. As the leader of Supero, John Davis was the only person to speak to The Enforcer on a regular basis. His identity remained a secret but he held the ultimate power in the group. He set the group's agenda and only intervened at crucial times. The Enforcer had final say on every decision. The man's secret identity had troubled John Davis since his acceptance into the group. He was told that the man's identity would forever remain a secret to insure that the group's core was never compromised. He did not know if The Enforcer was a current member or if he would forever remain invisible. He was intimidating and demanding.

"Sir, I would like to give you my deepest apology. It was never my intention to bring our group close to the public's eye. You must understand this."

"It is my duty as leader of this group to insure its safety and anonymity. You are never to speak of its existence even under the most dire consequences. You must be prepared to give up your life for our mission. I question your loyalty to our group."

"Sir, my loyalties are to our group. Our group comes before country and family to me. My actions were careless but our group was at the center of every action that was taken."

"You must cease any and all activity. There will be no revenge of any sort to any person. You must relay this message to our other members. For all intensive purposes our group will cease to exist until further notice. Is this understood?"

"Yes sir. I will relay your message through our communication network. All activity will cease immediately. I am prepared to give my life for our cause. Our group will prevail when the time is right."

The Enforcer did not respond. He simply hung up the phone on former President John Davis. Davis noticed that his hands were shaking when the call ended. Many considered him to be the most powerful man in the world but he knew that this was far from the truth. The Enforcer ultimately controlled the world. He did so very quietly, even within Supero. But he was the guiding hand behind the most powerful society in the world. And he would not allow the group to fold or encounter any major problems under any circumstances. John Davis had lost all power and he knew that it made him vulnerable. Many sleepless nights would ensue as he pondered what could be in store for him. He had failed the American people but more importantly in his mind, he had failed the secret society that he felt so honored to be a part of.

Daniel Worth broadcasted his thirty minute speech to the nation from his office in Charlotte. Everything was on the line as he would be spending the vast majority of his campaign budget on the speech. Primetime television coverage was not cheap but he knew that a well delivered speech could change the scope of next year's election. He wanted to have a conversation with the American people to let them know exactly what his plan was for the country. He would speak to them in specifics instead of the generalities that they had grown tired of. He dressed in a polo shirt and slacks, which was rather informal attire but he was trying to connect with real Americans. The four major networks had agreed to air the speech at a cost of over ten million dollars. It would be the defining moment of his campaign, win or lose. Wes Holland had been by his side for the past two weeks, enjoying the campaign and freedom. For the first time in weeks, he felt like he might have a future and he also felt like The New World Project was still a possibility. Senator Worth was calm and cool as the television cameraman gave him the signal to speak.

Chapter 30

"My fellow Americans, first of all I would like to thank you for taking time out of your busy schedules to tune in tonight. I come to you during an uncertain yet monumental period of our country's history. Many of you are hurting tonight, having either lost you job, lost your home, lost a great deal of your 401K investments or you may be worried about where you are going to find the money to pay next month's bills. Many of you have lost a great deal of confidence in your elected leaders and are uncertain of where our country is headed. I am here to tell the American people that it is time for a change. I am also here to tell you exactly how our country will change if I am elected as your next President."

"Many of you know that I have served in the Senate for the past eight years for the great state of North Carolina. I won my seat by running as an independent and as many of you know, I am running as an independent in the 2012 Presidential election. We have two major political parties in this country and they both have a storied history. Both parties have provided the balance and debate needed to take our country to heights that our forefathers never dreamed of. But we have reached a crossroads in this country. The divisiveness and bickering between the two parties has reached a level that is unhealthy. I know that many of you are tired of the rhetoric and I am here to change that. Our next President needs to have the ability to work with both parties to bring great change to this country. I can assure you that I have your best interest in mind, not the interests of donors or lobbyists. So I ask that you listen tonight with an open mind. I ask that you think about what is in the best interest of our country and make a decision based on the candidate that you think will bring us out of our current economic crisis. I want you to vote for the candidate that you think can bridge the widening gap between our political parties. And I ask that you vote for the candidate that you feel will change our direction and send us into the next decade prepared for growth and prosperity. I am going to tell you specifically how I plan to get us there and I will begin with a plan that will revolutionize not only our great country, but this plan will revolutionize the world."

"The New World Project will bring us out of our economic catastrophe, it will eliminate our national debt and it will put us back into the lead as the world's innovators. The New World Project is going to bring hundreds of thousands of manufacturing jobs back into our country and it will deliver a real transfer of wealth from oil companies to every working American household. The New World Project will end our dependence on foreign oil and it will reverse the very real trend of global warming. The New World Project will change this country for the better and it will be viewed as having as big of an impact as the automobile, the telephone and the computer."

"What is The New World Project you ask? It is a transportation system that will be implemented over the next five years that will run completely on electricity. Our current vehicles will be retrofitted to run on a track that will transport us to where we need to go for half the cost of gasoline and it will do so in a fraction of the time that it takes us today. The system will be run completely by computers so there will no longer be a need to drive. Car crashes will be a thing of the past. If you are a parent of a teenager watching tonight, you will no longer have the fear of your child being involved in a horrific alcohol related accident. Our people will be safer, we will get to where we need to go much quicker and every American family will save thousand of dollars each year in fuel costs. It will be a pay as you go system and it will be a real savings that gives you more discretionary income to spend on the things that you need to run your household."

"Oil companies will hate The New World Project because our country will be taking the billions in profit that oil companies earn each year and Americans will keep this money for themselves. Your income taxes will decline as The New World Project will generate the vast majority of the tax revenue that will be needed to fund the programs that keep our country running. The New World Project will pay for itself within two years and after that point the additional revenue will be used to pay off our national debt within a decade. We will sell the technology to every country around the world and our government will run on a surplus. We will take back our title as the dominant Super Power in the world and we will lead the parade to reverse global warming."

"Companies that create new manufacturing and customer service jobs in the United States will receive extremely beneficial tax breaks on transportation costs. We will bring back the jobs that my predecessors allowed us to lose and we will begin the process of rebuilding a strong and stabilizing middle class that has been the backbone of our country for decades. It is time for the United States of America to reclaim our role as the world's greatest manufacturers of products. It is time to bring back the millions of jobs that were lost. America, it is time for us to take our country back."

"The New World Project will create thousands of jobs during its construction. While the track is being built, there will be no major traffic delays. A six inch metallic strip will be built down the middle of every lane of every road in this country. It will be done with state of the art machinery that will build this project quickly, efficiently and cleanly. The cost of retrofitting your vehicles will be several hundred dollars each and you will be receiving a tax credit when the retrofit is complete. Auto manufacturers will turn into tram manufacturers. The technology to build a new tram will be simple and the trams will be extremely affordable to purchase."

"Imagine for a moment typing your destination into a computer then sitting back and enjoying your favorite television program while traveling at speeds of up to five hundred miles per hour to reach your destination. A family living on the east coast would be able to visit the west coast with a travel time of six hours and a travel cost of only two hundred dollars for the entire family. Americans will be able to visit areas of this great country that they never thought possible. Extended families will be reunited more frequently as the cost and speed of travel will diminish greatly. Tourism will boom as a weekend getaway can be something that all families can afford to enjoy. Sophisticated campgrounds will pop up all over the country for families that wish to travel but can not afford to stay in a hotel. Family trams will look like today's RV's but will cost a fraction of the price as there is no motor involved. Imagine traveling across the country within a matter of hours without having to go through the hassle of airport security."

"Americans will enjoy a much better quality of life when The New World Project becomes a reality. Millions of Americans endure stressful commutes today. The day in and day out grind of bumper to bumper traffic takes tolls on our bodies that no human should have to endure. Imagine a stress free drive to work everyday in a fraction of the time that it takes you now. You will be able to spend more time with your families each day and enjoy the quick trip to the office. The harmful chemicals that our automobiles emit today will be replaced by electricity that is powered by wind, solar, hydroelectric and nuclear power. Our air will be cleaner immediately and will only improve as time goes on. Asthma cases will dwindle as the air that we breathe will be fresh and clean."

"We can once again control our own financial destiny as oil producers will never hold us hostage again. The price of a barrel of oil has affected the stock market and our way of life for years and we can kiss that headache goodbye as we will produce the energy that transports us around this great country. Goods and services will be transported much more quickly, safely and efficiently than they ever have before. A package that must arrive five hundred miles away can do so in the same day. If you want take out from your favorite restaurant but it is fifty miles away, you will be able to order it and have it at your door in less than an hour. You can shop from the privacy of your home and get delivery the same day. The way that we operate is about to change and our country will be better for it."

"The New World Project comes to us at a time when this country direly needs it. We need to create new jobs, we need a real transfer of wealth that tax payers do not have to bank role, we need an economic boom to get us back on track and we direly need to clean up our environment so that we can leave our children with a cleaner planet than we inherited."

"I am proud and honored to be running for the office of President of the greatest nation in the world. My father served this country as a Senator for thirty years and he is my hero. He taught me everything that I know. He is a man of great character and great sacrifice. As I speak to you tonight, please understand that I realize and respect the scope of the job before me. I will work every day and night to keep our country safe and to make the United States of America the greatest country in the world. The middle class of this country is disappearing quickly and I realize that we must revitalize what has always been and will be the backbone of this country."

"Every American should have the opportunity to realize the American dream. We should be able to live in a country that is clean, safe and offers the opportunity for everyone to be successful, not just a chosen few. I want to lead this country on a journey of prosperity but I need your help to do it. We will survive this difficult time in our history and we will be stronger for having gone through it. God bless the great people of this country and God Bless America."

Chapter 31

The Enforcer watched the entire speech by Senator Daniel Worth very intently. The speech had gone exactly as he had expected it to. His photographic memory would not require that the speech be recorded or played over. He memorized every detail of the thirty minute broadcast as he viewed it. He felt the burden of a nation on his shoulders but more importantly it was his responsibility to guard a society more important than any one policy decision or event. Supero was bigger than its membership. Anything truly great was more important than its collective parts. The group had set the course of the world for decades and he would insure that the secret society would remain intact regardless of the scope of the obstacles that had to be over come.

He poured a glass of scotch on the rocks, opened his blinds to view the Capitol building and picked up his untraceable cell phone.

"The time has come" he said. "We are in code red."

I watched the speech from the luxury of my new apartment in Washington D.C. The apartment was a courtesy of the Worth campaign and I was working incredible hours while putting together the final touches of The New World Project. Senator Worth personally oversaw that all charges against me were dropped. Warren was exonerated from any wrong doing at the prison. And to my great relief, The New World Project was moving ahead at full speed. Senator Worth's job was to get elected while my job was to work with a team of scientists and engineers to plan the execution of the project should he be elected.

The first two weeks after my horrible ordeal were very difficult. I woke up in the middle of the night several times, drenched in sweat from nightmares that were reality only days before. I slept with the television turned on as it served as a kind of safety blanket as the background noise was a constant reminder that I was safe and free. Georgia Tech allowed me to take the semester off without penalty as they were enjoying more positive press than they had received in years. The brightest and most forward thinking high school minds in the country were now clamoring to attend the university. I even received a full pardon from my old roommate and we were back on regular speaking terms again. Megan and I were unable to get past the torment that she had been through but I did write her a lengthy letter with a very sincere apology that was well received.

Every day flew by as my dream was quickly becoming a workable plan. I met regularly with the heads of the Department of Transportation, auto executives, environmental experts and computer geniuses. My ordeal had changed me. Although I was much younger than everyone that I met, I was much more confident and demanding than I would have been before. I could see that my plan was a real possibility and I planned on seeing it through until the end.

Senator Worth did a fantastic job of selling the project to the American people. We had spent countless hours writing the speech and he delivered it in a way that made people realize the positive impact that the project would have on their lives. The Senator had found a new energy and drive with the discovery of a project that could change the way that the world lived. Professor Michaels had been correct. Daniel Worth was exactly the person that we needed to usher in the change that was required to make our dream a reality. His quiet sophistication and elegance allowed him to present such radical change in a way that made people feel comfortable and he assured them that it was the only path that our country needed to take. The Senator knew that the project would shape his Presidency and his legacy in the history books. He had an opportunity to be viewed as a savior when his country needed him the most. The fact that I had brought him the project put me into a position where I was treated like a king. Everyone that I met with treated me with respect. They knew that I was the brain behind the project and that working with me put them directly on the path to success. The entire scenario was setting up perfectly which made me a bit nervous given the recurring problems that had plagued me in the months prior.

CHAPTER 32

Former President John Davis watched the Worth speech alone in his home in Virginia. His wife continued her work with various charities that she had committed to before her husband's unfortunate demise. Davis was free to roam the grounds of his estate but was not allowed to leave the premises. It was very difficult for him to sit around with nothing to do as his entire working life had involved long hours, important decisions and stress that would put most men in the grave. To go from being the President of the United States to being under house arrest was torture for him. He did feel fortunate that the American people did not learn of his involvement with Supero. The people knew that he had embezzled money and that several of his wealthy and prominent friends had benefited. But thankfully that was the extent to which the network was exposed. He could live with impeachment as long as the most important society in the world was not discovered.

Davis could see the writing on the wall after the speech. Senator Worth was intelligent, handsome, witty and unfortunately very Presidential. There would need to be a major scandal for Worth not to be elected in a landslide victory. John Davis would have loved to plot his opponent's demise but he had quickly become inconsequential. When serving as President, he had hundreds of important friends with each pleading for a moment of his time. They all disappeared when the scandal broke. No one wanted to be connected to a criminal that had cheated his country out of millions of dollars. He had felt lonely when he was on the top of the world but he had no idea what loneliness was until he hit rock bottom. The Secret Service detail that had guarded his every move as President were now making sure that he did not leave the confines of his estate. There were days when he realized that things could be much worse but most of his time was spent regretting the moves that had caused his downfall. He was a lame duck with no future.

Former President Davis was depressed after the speech by Senator Worth and after flipping through the television menu, he decided to call it a night. His wife was attending a charity function in San Diego so he was alone. He set the security alarm, turned off all of the lights and made his way up to his second story bedroom. As he peered out his bedroom window, his entire estate was dark. A thick cloud cover blocked any illumination that the moon and stars would provide. It was his darkest hour. He brushed his teeth, used the bathroom, took one long look in the mirror at his aging face and flicked off the bathroom light as he made the familiar trip to his empty bed in complete darkness. The red illumination from the alarm clock was the only light in the room as he pulled back the sheets and comforter to crawl into bed.

He knew that something was wrong as soon as he slid his legs under the covers. His legs bumped into what felt like a large leather rope that had been left under the covers, but the rope was moving. He felt the pain immediately as he lunged for the switch on the lamp while kicking his legs ferociously out of instinct. The pain was sharp as fangs entered both legs in several locations. The rattlesnakes injected their venom immediately with strike after deadly strike. John Davis cried out in pain as he knocked over the table lamp and rolled out of his bed in the darkness. He crawled to the bathroom door which was about six feet away and sprang up on his knees to switch on the light. His fears were confirmed as he peered at his bed and saw several large rattlesnakes squirming around on his mattress. He immediately looked down at his legs and watched them swell before his very eyes. He had a tremendous fear of snakes and panic set in as his worst nightmare was coming true. There were more fang marks than he could count as the venom was racing to his vital organs. He limped his way across the room as quickly as his poison filled limbs would allow, careful to avoid the reptiles while searching for the telephone. He picked up the receiver while wincing in pain that was only getting worse. He knew that he was in dire straits when the phone had no dial tone. It was then that he knew the Enforcer had decided to dispose of him. He stumbled down the stairs, grabbed the keys to his car and crawled down the steps in front of his estate. John Davis never made it to his vehicle. His body would be discovered over an hour later only a few feet from his vehicle. The former president was dead.

Phil James, the CEO of World Airlines, was very disoriented when he woke up. The last thing that he remembered was walking out to his car to get his briefcase. His vision was blurred and he was freezing. For some reason, he was laying outside on the ground. He rubbed his eyes to try to bring his senses back to normal. His head was pounding from what felt like a hangover. As his vision returned, he only became more confused. His eyes began to adjust to the darkness and he realized that he was in what looked like a jungle. He could hear exotic birds singing in the distance. There appeared to be a viewing platform in the distance but he had no idea where he was. It looked like he was in an African plain but the plain was actually in a large enclosure. His footing was very unsteady as he rose to his feet. He took a long look around to try to get his bearings. He began the walk to the platform. He figured that would be the easiest way out of wherever he was.

The airline executive knew that getting up to walk was a mistake within the first thirty feet of his journey. His unsteady walk turned into an all out sprint as soon as he determined exactly where he was. As a cloud passed and the moon came into full view, Phil James got a clear glimpse of what he was up against. Unfortunately his movement had alerted his new enemy. Two very large and menacing Bengal tigers had seen him and were now stalking their prey. He didn't know whether to run or stand still but running put him farther away from the tigers. The huge cats were unhappy that they had an intruder and their natural instinct kicked into gear. They began their pursuit immediately and surrounded the helpless victim. One cat roared and it was a sound that could be heard throughout the zoo. Phil James froze in fear while trying to sweet talk the two ferocious predators. Phil James never had a chance. His mangled remains were found by zookeepers the next morning.

Walter Phelps, the wealthiest man in America, could live with the house arrest penalty that was imposed upon him. He was not allowed to leave his property in Colorado which was more than fine with him. He owned over ten thousand acres of beautiful Rocky Mountain wilderness. Since his arrest, he had been spending many nights camping on his property. He enjoyed the solitude of packing up a tent and venturing out into the wild. The fresh mountain air refreshed him and took him into a much more uncomplicated world than the one that he was accustomed to. He had become at one with nature and enjoyed avoiding the rest of the world. The man that could afford the most plush accommodations in the world slept best in a tent on the ground with a sleeping bag for a bed.

The first growl awoke him immediately. He knew that he had put his food away but the roar of a grizzly bear was unmistakable. He unzipped the inside of his tent to peer through the screen. The illumination from the dwindling campfire provided all of the light that he needed. Food had been scattered throughout the campsite and a family of large grizzlies was now scavenging the site. Phelps froze in fear when he noticed a blood trail that led directly to the front of his tent. He was unarmed and helpless as he eased the zipper closed and backed his way to the very middle of his canvas entrapment. He was silent and terrified as the family of bears plodded around the campsite.

He had no idea how the food had been scattered and no clue as to how a blood trail could possibly lead to his tent. He had been sleeping for several hours without a sound outside of his tent. His heart raced as he prayed for the nightmare to end. The roar of a grizzly outside of his tent paralyzed the billionaire. He was trapped with nowhere to go. When the first claw crashed down on him he knew that it was only a matter of time. He was blinded by his canvas tent and fought for as long as he could but Walter Phelps did not survive. His remains were found the next morning by a passing hiker.

Dave Nelson swore that he must be dreaming or simply imagining things. He had fallen asleep in his Malibu mansion after a long night of drinking whiskey sours. He had been confined to his home for almost two weeks and with no visitors allowed, he was going stir crazy. The wealthy entrepreneur awoke from his drunken slumber tied to the side of his yacht, with his legs dangling in the water. The roar of the engine brought him into reality as the boat was miles from shore and moving at a high rate of speed. His mouth was gagged and his hands were dangling above his head, not allowing him to escape. After about twenty minutes, the boat came to a sudden stop. The lower half of his body rested in the water as ropes that held his arms kept his upper half above the water. After sitting for several minutes in darkness, a spot light suddenly illuminated the ocean. He could not speak and could not turn his body to see who was on the yacht. He tried with all of his might to pull himself up but his arms were spread far apart and each attempt only exhausted him more. Suddenly there were splashes all around him as someone was throwing bloody chum into the water. Tears began steaming down his face as his legs tried violently to find fresh air.

The first fin appeared after several minutes then it was joined by what appeared to be an army of fins. Within seconds of sensing the fresh blood, a swarm of sharks were in a feeding frenzy. The ocean around Dave Nelson became a chaotic pool of gnashing teeth. Dave Nelson was dead.

Bob Blanton, the oil tycoon from Texas, had spent the past two weeks in the penthouse of a high rise condo building that he owned in Gulf Shores Alabama. Due to his house arrest, he was unable to leave the property, which was exactly why he had chosen his condo on the Gulf Coast. He had access to three swimming pools, two hot tubs, tennis courts, two five star restaurants and maid service. The penthouse was all windows and since it took up the entire top floor of the building, he had a panoramic view of the area. He spent his mornings drinking coffee on the large balcony that overlooked the water while searching for dolphins and listening to the waves pound the shoreline. His house arrest had turned into a much needed vacation away from the grind of the Texas oil fields.

Blanton was sitting outside on the balcony at 11:00 P.M. when he heard room service enter his suite for turn down service and a new bottle of scotch.

"Just sit it on top of the bar" he commanded through the open screened door on the balcony.

"Yes sir. May I pour you a drink while I am here?" the attendant asked.

"Sure son, that would be fantastic. I'll take a scotch on the rocks. Are you new? I haven't seen you up here before."

"Yes sir. I've been on the job for about a week."

The attendant mixed the drink and took it out to Blanton who was eagerly waiting on the balcony.

"Son, I will tip you next time. My wallet is in the bedroom and I'm too damn old to get up."

"A tip will not be required sir."

John and Susan McCann were enjoying a long weekend away from the kids. John's boss had a condo on the Gulf Coast and was nice enough to let them use it for the weekend. The time away from the kids was exactly what they needed. They were on drink number four and enjoying the hot tub as a cool breeze blew off of the Gulf waters. There was no one else in the darkened pool area so Susan decided to surprise John and took off her bathing suit top. She turned to John with a smile on her face and handed him her top. John didn't know what to say as it had been years since his wife was this daring.

They both turned their heads simultaneously when they heard the crashing sound. The splat was like nothing either of them had ever heard. The sound of crushing bones was grotesque. The body fell only ten feet from where they were sitting. The bathing suit top went on immediately and they scurried for help. Bob Blanton did not survive the fall.

Fahim Al Zahrani enjoyed many of the perks of being filthy rich. One perk that he really enjoyed was his ability to purchase the accompaniment of beautiful young women, particularly blond American women. He found blond Americans fascinating and he was very excited about the latest arrangement that his assistant had put together. Her name was Courtenay and she was gorgeous. She was fit, had beautiful brown eyes, was very curvy and originally from New Jersey. He was to meet her at his palace for dinner.

After a five course meal and two bottles of wine, Fahim showed Courtenay to his bedroom. There was a prearranged understanding about what was expected but Courtenay was to receive a handsome sum of cash at the end of the evening.

"Courtenay, please make yourself comfortable while I change."

His date did exactly as he asked by taking off the low cut cocktail dress that she had been wearing to reveal a see through black lingerie top and bottom. She laid on the bed awaiting his arrival.

"You are stunningly beautiful" he said as he entered the room in a bathrobe and laid down next to her on the bed, almost unable to contain himself.

"No. No. No. You can't touch yet" she said while pulling a blindfold out from her bra.

"I love you American women" he said with a sheepish grin.

"Have you been a bad boy Fahim?" she playfully asked.

"Yes, I have been very bad. How do you plan to punish me?

"I'm going to torture you" she replied. "Do you like torture Fahim?"

"Oh no. Please don't torture me" he said as his excitement continued to build.

Courtenay pulled out a pair of handcuffs.

"Give me one arm" she said forcefully.

Fahim immediately complied and she cuffed one of his hands to the headboard.

"Now I am going to blindfold you."

"If you must."

"Now Fahim, I have a little surprise for you. Reach into my purse. Do it now!"

Fahim did as he was told and felt around the bed for a purse. As he slid his hand from right to left, he stumbled upon a cloth sack. With his one free hand he opened the sack and reached in but the surprise was not what he was looking for.

"Courtenay, what is this?"

He would receive no response. Courtenay was long gone. Those were the last words that he spoke as a King Cobra found its target and ended the life of Fahim Al Zahrani.

CHAPTER 33

After a long but exciting day of meetings, Wes Holland returned to his apartment in Washington D.C. with Chinese takeout. His plan was to watch a new episode of The Office, slowly devour his beef and broccoli with fried rice and wind down after a hard day's work. His life was not normal but had become very exciting. Every day brought new and rewarding challenges but he was always happy every evening for some down time so that he could relax. He felt safe and he felt important. He had always wondered what true happiness felt like and he now understood.

A news flash appeared just minutes before his favorite program was to begin.

"We are interrupting this regularly scheduled program to bring you a special news report."

The leader anchor for NBC appeared and the look on his face was one of shock. It was not often that a lead anchor was frazzled, so whatever was happening had to be big.

"Ladies and gentlemen, we come to you tonight with some very tragic news. We are now a country in mourning as former President John Davis was found dead in his home tonight, the victim of a fatal snake bite. We have been sitting on this story for almost an hour by request of the White House. The official word is that as former President Davis was getting into bed tonight, he was bitten multiple times by several rattlesnakes. This story is extremely suspicious and authorities have not ruled out foul play. As most of you know, the former President was removed from office less than two weeks ago amid allegations of money laundering and the conspiracy to commit murder. It is too early to speculate, but I can not imagine a scenario where this occurred naturally. There is more to this story than we know and we are committed to getting to the bottom of it."

"This appears to be a savage and disgusting act by someone to get revenge on the President. There is no way to know at this time who is behind this despicable act. Please wait just one moment as we are getting new information."

The anchor paused as a huge knot appeared in Wes's stomach. Who in the world could be behind this? Who would want to kill the former President?

The anchor returned with a confused look on his face. "Ladies and gentlemen, this story is getting more bizarre by the minute. It appears as though we can now confirm that the former President was in fact murdered along with seven other members of the so called "Narcissistic Nine." To remind you, the Narcissistic Nine is the name that we have pinned on the nine men accused of laundering money from our government along with other charges. This group includes many of the wealthiest and most powerful men in the world. We are working to confirm each story as it comes across the news desk but this is very disturbing indeed."

"Not only have these men been murdered tonight, but the manner in which these atrocious acts have been committed is nothing less than disgusting. If you have young children that are watching this broadcast, we would ask that they leave the room now. The news that we are about to report is extremely graphic in nature. The nature in which these crimes were committed seems like something straight out of a mafia movie. I am going to run down this unbelievable list. In addition to former President Davis's grizzly murder, we now have reports that Dave Nelson, the young and extremely successful entrepreneur was found dead by coast guard officials off of the coast of California. The Coast Guard received a distress call and upon arrival found Nelson dangling from his yacht, his body half eaten by sharks. Folks, I am not making this up and I am going to continue. If you have a weak stomach, you may want to turn the channel."

"Bob Blanton, the popular Texas oil man, appears to have either jumped or been thrown off of the roof of a skyscraper tonight. I believe that it is safe to say at this point that he did not fall off of the side of the building on his own volition. His body was found in a small fountain in front of a building in Gulf Shores, Alabama. Many of you know Blanton for the generous contributions that he made to the athletics department of his alma mater, the University of Texas."

"The grim news keeps coming into the newsroom tonight as the mauled body of Phil James, the CEO of airline giant World Airlines, was found in the tiger exhibit of Zoo Atlanta. Zoo officials believe that James was lowered into the exhibit by helicopter as there was no sign of forced entry into the exhibit. The two Bengal tigers have been put down after the incident and zoo officials are very distraught. The official word from Zoo Atlanta is that there is no possible way that a human can enter the exhibit without official access. I can not imagine the extreme horror that James experienced in the moments before his death. It is surreal."

"The next victim of this horrible and obvious assassination plot is Bill Douglas, the auto executive from Detroit. Douglas burned to death tonight in a car fire. He was apparently forcibly tied down in the driver's seat of his SUV when the car was doused with some type of explosive material. His remains have not actually been identified but the family spokesperson has confirmed that the victim was in fact Douglas."

"We have received word from the family of billionaire Walter Phelps that his body was found this evening, the victim of an attack by grizzly bears. Phelps was camping alone on his property in Colorado and a hiker stumbled upon his remains this morning. Many of you know Walter Phelps as the wealthiest man in the world. Phelps was also the most generous man in the world in terms of the amount of money that he donated to charity. Our country and the world has been dealt a tremendous blow with his passing. Walter was a personal friend of mine and despite the allegations that have been levied upon him, I can tell you from personal experience that he was a great man and I am a better person for having known him."

"We do have confirmation from the Al Zahrani family in Saudi Arabia that Fahim Al Zahrani, who had recently taken over the family oil business, was the victim of a cobra bite in his home in Saudi Arabia. He did not survive the attack."

"And last but certainly not least, the Chinese government has confirmed that officials have found the body of Jun Wu, the Chinese Minister of Commerce. Wu was the victim of a hanging in his apartment in Beijing. As further details of his death emerge, we will bring you that information."

"It is difficult to speculate on why these horrific murders occurred tonight but one can only ascertain that the deaths of these influential men have something to do with the crimes in which they are linked. The White House is not providing additional information regarding the crimes in which these men are charged. Whether the deaths are some type of revenge for the wrongs committed or a way to keep the information secret will be discussed for years. But one thing is certain, what occurred tonight required a tremendous amount of manpower, money and sophistication. These crimes were not committed by amateurs. The assassinations of these men were committed by a group with military like expertise. We did not just find their bodies. A brutal and horrific message was intended to be sent."

"I'm going to bring in my co-anchor Stan Ryan to help us bring the events of tonight into perspective. Stan, please give us your thoughts on the impact that tonight will have on our country."

Stan Ryan, a thirty year veteran of NBC appeared on the screen. "First of all, I would like to send my condolences to the families and friends of these men. There is no doubt that our country will be affected by the events of tonight for years to come. We are talking about a combined wealth of many billions of dollars. It will be interesting to see how Wall Street reacts on Monday morning. This group collectively controlled many of the most recognizable brands in the world. The markets reacted very negatively when they were charged with several crimes and I believe that we can expect another plunge on Monday morning. My second observation revolves around the chilling way in which these men were killed. It sounds like a scene from a horror movie. If you sat around and tried to dream up the most brutal ways to kill a group of people, you could not top what occurred here tonight. It is frightening to know that someone could dream this up, much less pull it off."

John Mills, the anchor of NBC news returned to the screen. "There is one member of the Narcissistic Nine that is unaccounted for. Jeff Bates, the Wall Street Investment Banker, is unaccounted for. Law enforcement officials went to his home tonight when word of the fate of the other men was learned. Bates, who was not allowed to leave his residence due to this house arrest, was not home when officials arrived. We can only hope and pray that Mr. Bates is safe tonight. There is a nationwide search underway for Mr. Bates and we will keep you updated as soon as we learn anything. Please tune in at 10:00 eastern time tonight for an hour long special on the tragedies of tonight. We are going to spend the next two hours putting our hands around this entire situation and bring you everything that we know at that time. Until then, we ask that you pray for the victims families in this difficult time. We now return you to your regularly scheduled program."

Wes stared wide eyed and in disbelief at the television screen. His dinner was untouched and the fear that had finally left him returned instantly. He dialed his brother.

"Will, are you watching the news?"

"Unfortunately I am. What is the world is going on?"

"I have no earthly idea. I know that someone wants to shut those guys up, but who could it be?"

"Do you think that it could be the government?" Will asked.

"God I hope not but that is not as crazy as it sounds. Think about it. They know that if word of Supero ever reached the public, there would be riots in the streets. If the plots that this group was planning ever became known, we would have another Civil War."

"I don't want to scare you Wes, but if this theory is true, then you could be in danger again. I don't think that the government is behind this, but you never know. I don't know what to think anymore."

"You and me both. But I don't think it's the government. I just don't see how they would murder that group of people regardless of what they were plotting."

"Well, someone wanted them dead so you need to watch your back."

"I'm going to call Senator Worth in the morning and see if he can't arrange protection for me."

"That's not a bad idea."

The knock on Wes's apartment door made him jump to attention.

"Hey, I've got to go, someone's at the door."

"Be careful man. Do you want me to stay on the phone until you see who it is?"

"You're in Kentucky. There's not a whole lot you can do. I'll be fine and besides, if someone wanted to kill me I don't think they would knock."

Wes hung up with his brother then folded up the uneaten cartons of Chinese food and threw them in the half empty fridge. He could not believe his eyes when he peered through the hole in his front door. His adrenaline started racing and he ran to the kitchen and grabbed his largest butcher knife. Life was getting too interesting very quickly. He opened the door but kept the chain fastened so that he could speak through the hole.

"What do you want?" he asked.

"I know that you are probably shocked to see me and I will completely understand if you turn your back on me, but you are my only chance to stay alive. Will you please let me in to explain myself? I'm unarmed, I swear" Jeff Bates whispered as he took off his coat and spun completely around.

"You've got five minutes and then you are getting the hell out of here" Wes answered while unlocking the chain and opening the door. "Come on in and have a seat on the couch. I guess I don't need to tell you what has been going on tonight."

"No you don't. I have been living in my D.C. home since the arrest and once I heard that President Davis was murdered I slipped out. Wes, I don't deserve your help but I'm going to ask for it anyway. I'm a dead man if I try to run. Will you please talk to Senator Worth for me and try to get me some help."

"Why didn't you just go to the police?"

"I don't know who is behind this. I know that you have seen the tapes. It could be anyone that is after us."

"Who do you think it is?" Wes asked.

Jeff Bates squirmed in his seat and became very fidgety. He didn't want to answer the question.

"Listen man, I can't help you if you don't tell me. I have no stake in this. I've been in enough crap over the past few months and I don't want to get in the middle of this. You tried to have me killed. I have no problem putting you out on your butt right now. So either talk or get out."

Jeff Bates closed his eyes and took a deep breath.

"I believe that I know who it is. Supero has a leader."

"Yeah, it was President Davis. He's dead. Move on."

"No. There was someone above him. They called him the Enforcer. I only spoke with him once and it was by phone when I was accepted into the group. I know very little about him accept that he oversaw the entire operation. I have no idea who he is or where he lives. All that I know is that everyone and I mean everyone was intimidated by him."

"Even the President?"

"Especially the President because he was the only member of the group that dealt with the Enforcer on a regular basis."

"Why do you think it is him that is behind this?"

"Because the number one rule of Supero was that the group could never be made public. Supero was to be put above family, work, everything. Every member clearly understood that if the group was ever jeopardized, then every member's life was at stake."

"And you think that since the tape was made public, that this Enforcer guy decided to shut everyone up."

"Yes."

"And the Enforcer had the final say in every decision then?" Wes asked.

"I don't think so. The Enforcer oversaw the entire operation and was kept in the loop on decisions but I don't think that he made every decision. But something happened towards the end. It was more than just the fact that the tape was found. Something President Davis did really angered the Enforcer."

"And that is why he came after you?"

"Yeah, that and the fact that the tapes were made."

"So how can I help you?" Wes asked.

"I need for Senator Worth to protect me" Bates answered.

"What did the Enforcer say to you when you spoke with him?" Wes asked.

"Well, I have only been in the group for three years. Whenever someone new is accepted, the Enforcer has an introductory conversation with them. It is not really a hello, glad to have you kind of speech. It was more about the responsibility that you accept when you enter the group. He spoke about how the future of the world depended upon Supero. He spoke about loyalty, secrecy and the consequences that could result from talking about the group. I can remember it like it was yesterday. He said that true honor is achieved through sacrifice to something greater than yourself. He said that was the creed that he lived by and that was the creed of Supero.. The saying itself is not that creepy but the way that he said it made you know that you were handing your life over to this group."

"True honor is achieved through sacrifice to something greater than your-self" I repeated.

"They did a hell of a sales job on me. I bought into the group hook, line and sinker. And they truly felt that Supero should in fact run the world. To be honest, the group did control all major decisions that have been made since I have been a member."

"The entire premise is disgusting" Wes proclaimed.

"Yes it was. And I knew that. At least over the past six months or so. The first couple of years, the group did not do anything that was disgusting. But John Davis changed and Supero was not a democracy. To speak out against his ideas was a death sentence. I was stuck and there was nothing that I could do. I have a family and as bad as it sounds, I was not going against the group. I was too scared about what could happen. And my role was being the money guy. I moved money around the world for everyone including myself. And we got filthy rich off of it. I guess that I sold it to myself by saying that I wasn't actu-ally making the terrible decisions."

"I'm not going to judge you. It doesn't matter what I think anyway. I do have one question for you though. How did you find me?"

"The power of the internet. It is a pretty scary thing. Listen Wes, I don't want to bother you or put you in danger, but can I crash here tonight? I don't have anywhere to go and I swear that I will be out of here as soon as you talk to Daniel Worth."

"I guess you can stay here but it is one night only. That's it. And I don't want you even getting near a window. You have caused me enough turmoil for one lifetime."

CHAPTER 34

"Senator Worth, it's Wes."

"Hey Wes. I was going to call you this morning. You must be pretty nervous after what happened last night."

"You don't know the half of it."

"Talk to me buddy."

"Well yes, I was freaked out when I heard the news. But it reached an entirely new level when Jeff Bates showed up at my doorstep."

"Come again?"

"Jeff Bates is here at my apartment. Somehow he found me last night and said that I was the only person that he could think of to help him. I let him stay here last night but I don't want him anywhere around me. He is scared to death and doesn't know who to trust but he knows that he can trust you. He needs somewhere to hide. Can you help him?"

"Why do our conversations end up in places like this?"

"I don't know. All that I want to do is work on my project but trouble seems to keep finding me."

"Well I'm not going to let the guy die. I will have someone pick him up in fifteen minutes. I'm sorry about this Wes."

"It's not your fault. Hey, are you still going to be able to make it to the test run tomorrow?"

"I wouldn't miss is for the world. And Wes, I am going to assign a security team to you. It is against policy but yesterday's events allow me to break protocol. I want you concentrating on the New World Project and nothing else."

"Thanks Senator."

"Would you quit calling me that. It's Daniel."

"Hopefully soon it will be Mr. President."

The day that I had been waiting for was finally here. A private plane took my team of engineers to west Texas where the first trial run of the New World Project would take place. We laid forty miles of track below Amarillo to test our system. We retro-fitted forty old vehicles to run on the track and installed computers in each of them. I was the lead on the project and addressed the team of twenty before we began. The excitement was impossible to contain as the sun rose above the eastern horizon. I was extremely nervous because I wanted everything to go off without any major snags.

I took the podium at 7:30 A.M.

"First of all, I would like to thank each of you for your efforts on this project. Today we will conduct stage one testing of the New World Project. We all know what is at stake here today. We are going to change the world together and I would be remiss not to mention that this dream was born in the office of a very dear friend, the late Harold Michaels. Professor Michaels made my dream a reality and it is in his honor that we begin this testing today. This project is my life's work and there were many nights when I thought that it would never get off of the ground. But with all of your help, we have made it a reality and within five years, this transportation system will completely change our world. Let's get to work."

Daniel Worth, Sue Michaels and myself got into what used to be a Honda Accord. We entered our destination into the computer and sat back to enjoy the ride. As the vehicle started its journey, tears streamed down my cheeks. The round trip was eighty miles and we were back at the starting point within fifteen minutes. The project was off and running. The first test run was a success!

Jeff Bates contacted his wife who was staying with relatives. The Secret Service had taken him to a hotel and would watch over him until further notice. He was frightened but feeling better about his situation since he was no longer on the run. After unpacking the small backpack that he had grabbed in his rush to leave his home, he decided to unwind and take a long hot shower. He avoided the television because he did not need constant reminders of the fate of his fallen comrades. He understood the seriousness of his predicament and he also knew that until the Enforcer was captured, his life was in danger. His wife was panicked when they talked. She did not understand what was happening and would never know the full details of why he was being hunted. As he dried off from his shower and put on a pair of gym shorts and a tee shirt, a sudden wave of paranoia overcame him.

As he entered the living area of the suite which he had been given, his worst nightmare was realized. Sitting on the couch with gun in hand was the Enforcer himself.

Jeff Bates did not need an explanation. He simply stared at the man in disbelief.

"It's you? You are the Enforcer?"

"Yes Jeff, it is me. Are you surprised?" the Enforcer said while flashing an evil smile.

"I must say that I am." Bates was dejected. He had no weapon or form of defense. He was an investment banker with no self defense skills. The closest that he ever came to violence was a two year stint on his high school lacrosse team.

"Jeff, the group has been compromised. I guess that I don't need to tell you that. You must realize that what has happened was inevitable. When you took the oath to become a member of the most exclusive club in the world, you knew that this ending was a possibility."

"Sir, may I ask how you got passed the Secret Service detail?"

"You can ask, but you will not get an answer."

"Is there anything in the world that I can do? It doesn't have to end this way. I will take my secrets to the grave, Sir. I promise you that I will. Is there any amount of money that I can give you? I will do anything to survive."

The Enforcer stared at Jeff Bates then started an evil laugh that became hysterical. Bates stood in his gym shorts, unable to move. He had no plan. There was no exit strategy. He was on the fourteenth floor for his safety so there was no escape.

"Sir, is there anything that I can do?"

The laugh immediately turned into a snarl with eyes that pierced directly into Jeff Bates soul.

"I knew when we let you in the group that you were weak. Only a weak man would beg for his life. Supero is bigger than you Jeff. Supero is bigger than any one man. Its survival is more important than any single event. So your answer is no, there is nothing that you can do to prevent your death. True honor is achieved through sacrifice to something greater than yourself."

The Enforcer raised the handgun with silencer attached and shot Jeff Bates four times in the chest. Death was immediate. The Enforcer wiped the gun down and quietly exited the way that he had entered, through the adjoining suite. Jeff Bates, the final living member of the Narcissistic Nine was dead.

Daniel Worth requested that I sit with him on the plane ride back to Washington. I was riding a wave of elation as the testing for the New World Project had gone better than we ever could have expected. As I found my seat next to the Senator, his expression was blank.

"Is something wrong Daniel?" I asked.

"Jeff Bates is dead. The Secret Service found him this afternoon in his hotel room. He was shot four times at point blank range."

"Oh no."

"Oh no is right. Wes, it had to be an inside job. There is no other way. There are only a few people who knew his location so I just can not figure out how this person got to them."

"It must be the Enforcer that he was telling me about."

"Whoever it was has some pretty powerful friends. I feel terrible about this. He came to me for protection and he is dead within a few hours after entering our custody."

"Listen Daniel, I don't want to add to your stress but you and I could be next on the list."

"I have already thought of that. And I am in the middle of a campaign so hiding out is not an option. I am pretty spooked by the whole thing."

"So am I. I finally got to a point where the nightmares were going away and now this. We know way too much for this Enforcer guy to be comfortable with us."

"All that I can do is put as much security around us as possible and hope for the best."

"Or catch this maniac."

"Believe me, we have our best special ops guys on the case but I am at a point where I don't know who to trust and who not to trust. It's tough to even gauge what is real and what isn't real."

"I know. Welcome to my world. We have got to find this guy. It is obviously someone that has a lot of connections. Someone that knows the inner workings of government" Wes said.

"We will find him and we will bring him to justice."

"I just hope that you and I are around to see it."

"We will be Wes. And hey, I don't mean to be dumping my frustrations out on you. It just gets kind of lonely from the seat that I am sitting in. And there are not many people that I can confide in on situations like this one."

"I completely understand Daniel."

CHAPTER 35

Inauguration Day – January 20, 2017

Location – Lincoln Memorial, Washington D.C.

A crowd of over one million people came to see the inauguration of their new President, Daniel Worth. Crowds began forming around the reflection pool hours before sunrise. Wes Holland would sit within ten feet of the newly elected President and would remain in Washington to lead the New World Project. Optimism was at a ten year high as the United States had elected the first independent President in the country's history. Daniel Worth won the election in a landslide victory. After taking the oath of office, President Worth addressed the crowd.

"My fellow Americans, I am humbled to have the opportunity to serve this great country for the next four years. As I speak to you today, I know that many of you are hurting. Millions of you are out of work, out of money and out of time. While traveling throughout this great country of ours, I have heard you loud and clear. It is time for change in America and the change starts today."

The crowd let out a round of applause that could be heard for miles as the President waited to continue.

"I realize that the mountain that we must climb is steep. There is no time to waste and every step that we take must be the right one. Throughout the history of this great country, we have faced many obstacles. At every turning point, the great people of this country have risen above whatever obstacle was thrown in our way and we have prevailed as a stronger nation. This critical time in our history will be no different. We will come together now and we will start the healing process. We are going to change the world that we live in for the better and that change starts today!"

The crowd once again let out a resounding round of applause as the President gathered his thoughts.

"Over the past ten years we have stood by and watched as hundreds of thousands of good paying jobs have been moved overseas. We stood by and watched as the backbone of our country, the hard working middle class, has been decimated. My fellow Americans we will stand by and watch no more! We will bring your jobs back to the United States and that process begins today."

The crowd began a chant of "Daniel Worth, Daniel Worth."

"My friends, today is not a day to assign blame. Today is a day to start anew. It doesn't matter what your background is. It doesn't matter how much money you make. It doesn't matter what color your skin may be. And it doesn't matter what your belief system is. Because today we stand together as one nation, with one common purpose."

"Today is the day that we begin the process of fixing this great country of ours. We are Americans and that is what we do!"

The crowd went wild with chants of "USA, USA, USA."

"Today we will begin the process of cleaning our air. Today we will accept responsibility for the damage that technology has caused to our planet. We do not place blame on our past advancements, we simply keep advancing. We will leave future generations with a sustainable environment. We are going to clean the air that is making so many of our children sick and within five years we will completely end our dependence on foreign oil."

"We will not completely shut out our friends from other countries that are manufacturing goods for us. But starting today, made in the USA is going to mean something again. We will work with the many great brands across this country to create good new manufacturing jobs right here, today."

"My friends, there was a day not too long ago when we were on the cutting edge of inventing the products that make our world a better place. We have slipped in technological development but that changes today."

The crowd shouted "Today."

"There was a time not long ago when this great country did not have a deficit that seemed insurmountable. There was a time that many of us remember when the people of this great country were not in debt up to their eyeballs. When people did not have a wallet full of maxed out credit cards. And when people worked and saved their money before making a purchase. My fellow Americans, we are going to fix this financial mess that we have created for ourselves starting today."

The crowd once again shouted "Today."

"We are going to refocus ourselves to educate our children, teach them right from wrong and bring fiscal discipline back into our homes. In order for us to accomplish this goal, I need you America. I need you to take a look back at your grandparent's generation, the greatest generation. They were a people that did not live for material things. Our grandparent's generation valued what really mattered in life. They valued family, good hard honest work and true friendship with their neighbors. We have made mistakes, there is no doubt about it. But if we roll our sleeves up and get to work, this country will reach highs that we could never dream of. People, we can't wait until tomorrow, we have got to start today."

One million people shouted at the top of their lungs "Today."

"We are all in agreement that we must create jobs, we must operate our government with a balanced budget, we must improve the quality of the air that we breathe and we must cement our position as the premier innovators in this world that we live in. How are we going to do that you ask? The answer is the New World Project. I am joined here today with a very dear friend by the name of Wes Holland. Wes's dream was to create a transportation system that is far superior to the system that we currently use. Wes has dedicated his life to making that dream a reality. And with the help of hundreds of talented scientists and engineers, within five years the New World Project will be a reality. This project will create thousands of jobs immediately, it will end our dependence on foreign oil and the way that we transport ourselves around this great country of ours will take a leap forward that many never dreamed possible. Moving from place to place will be a pleasure instead of a burden. Tens of thousands of lives will be saved each year because there will be no more car crashes, there will be no more wear and tear on our bodies from the stresses of driving, there will be no more alcohol related vehicle tragedies and emergency personnel will be able to respond to disasters in a fraction of the time that it takes them now. The air that we breathe will be clean and we can say goodbye to many of the respiratory illnesses that plague us today. Goods will move around this country so quickly that we will reinvent commerce as we know it. We will sell this technology to the world and erase the federal deficit that seems insurmountable to us today. We will run our government on a surplus while greatly reducing your tax burden. We will retrofit your vehicles to run on this system and we will do it cheaply. The cost of travel will be cut in half and you will be able to travel around this country with an ease and speed that seems impossible today. This system will bring families together more often and it will allow millions to see this beautiful country of ours at a fraction of the what it costs you now. Tourism will boom, commerce will boom and my friends, this nation will boom."

The crowd roared.

"This is not a dream, it is a reality. We are going to improve our environment, take care of our fiscal obligations, put more money into every family's pockets and show the world that the United States of America can offer them a better way of life."

"Friends, I realize that many of you have grown to be leery of your country's leadership. I also realize that for me to gain your trust, it must be earned over time. I will dedicate my life to gaining that trust. And together we are about to embark on a journey that many generations will look back on with pride. When we are all gone, we will leave behind a legacy that future generations will work to live up to. The time is now, not tomorrow, not next week and not next year. The work begins today. And if we all come together we will right our wrongs immediately. I ask for your patience, I ask for your support and I ask for your prayers as we begin this wonderful journey"

"I want to leave you today with a saying that is the mantra of someone that I hold very dear to my heart, my father. My father is a man that has dedicated his life to serving this great country of ours. He says that true honor is achieved through sacrifice to something greater than yourself. That is a wonderful way to live life. So I ask you today to join me on this journey. May God bless you and may God bless America."

CHAPTER 36

That phrase, I know that phrase. Where did I hear it? My brain was racing as I sat in front of over a million people with television cameras showing me in the background. On no! Oh God! I knew that phrase. Jeff Bates uttered it to me on the night before he died. It was the motto that the Enforcer lived by.

The greatest day of my life turned into the worst when the final words of our new President's speech rolled off of his tongue. I could not hide the shock that ran through my body when I discovered where I had heard it. I was paralyzed as a chill ran through my bones. I sat in my chair with my hands on my face as everyone else was on their feet, applauding and cheering their new leader. I did hear the mantra correctly, didn't I? As much as I wanted to deny knowing the phrase, deep down I now knew who the Enforcer was. This was bad and it was only going to get worse.

As Daniel Worth and his family exited to cheering crowds, I stood and stared at his father. The old man looked proud of his only son. I stared into his eyes and could feel the evil in his heart. He was the leader of the biggest conspiracy that this world has ever known and it culminated with his son being elected as the leader of the free world. His reign of terror was only beginning. The names of the members of the group would change but his stronghold on controlling the world was as strong as ever. Senator George Worth, a lifetime veteran of the Senate had been living a double life for almost thirty years. He appeared to be a conservative grandfatherly type of leader when in actuality he was leading a group so evil and so powerful that even the leader of the free world could not escape its wrath.

My mind was racing as I shook hands and tried to play the part of an elated member of the new President's cabinet. A day that had started with so much promise had quickly deteriorated into yet another roadblock in my path to having a normal life. My life was still in danger. And I wasn't sure if Daniel Worth was in on his father's true identity. Were they just keeping me as a pawn to be used until my purpose was fulfilled? Was the man that I had entrusted my life to only playing me? There were so many more questions than answers and I began to feel ill. I had to get to the bottom of this but inauguration day would make the new President almost impossible to access.

There would be about an hour before an inaugural luncheon that I was required to attend so I called the only person that I knew I could trust.

"Will, do you have a minute?"

"Hey, I'm glad that you are still speaking to your lowly brother. I saw you on television. That had to be the coolest thing that I have ever seen in my life. How does it feel to be a celebrity?"

"Will, I've got some bad news."

"What now? What could possibly be going wrong now? Do not give me bad news today."

"Do you remember the end of Daniel's speech, when he quoted his father's mantra?"

"Yes, he said something about how you achieve true honor."

"He said that true honor is achieved through sacrifice to something greater than yourself."

"And what is wrong with that?"

"Well, I haven't told you this but the day before Jeff Bates died, he came to my apartment."

"Do what?"

"He was on the run and didn't know who else could help him so he tracked me down. I've been keeping this from you because I don't want you to worry. He said that Supero had a leader, someone called the Enforcer. He said that the Enforcer only spoke to the group by phone and Bates had only actually spoken to this man once. He told me exactly what the man said and one of the things that he mentioned was the exact quotation that Daniel Worth quoted today."

"So you think that his dad is the leader of Supero."

"I don't think that he is. I know he is. What I don't know is if his son is involved."

"Wes, are you sure that you aren't being paranoid? Listen buddy, you have been through a lot lately."

"It was the exact quotation. Word for word."

"Oh Lord, Wes. Just when I think that you are safe, something else pops up. What are you going to do?"

"I have no idea. That's why I'm calling you. The President will be impossible to get to today. He's got a super tight schedule and I don't want to ruin the biggest day of his life."

"What if he is involved?" Will asked.

"I don't know. I just want to get out of here. I want to run and never enter this city again."

"That would be a bad move."

"What do I do?"

"Can you pin down the old man? See if you can get him to talk?"

"I don't know. This whole thing has me scared to death. If the old man really is the one in charge, I know that he has plans to kill me. And what if his son is in on it? I'm screwed. I dodged one President but there is no way that I could elude another one. And I'm tired of running. I can't do this anymore."

"I'll be thinking about you. Just let me know if there is anything that I can do. Would you like for me to get on a plane?"

"No, you just stay where you are and I will call you if I need you."

CHAPTER 37

Inaugural Luncheon

Capitol Building, Washington D.C.

I was trying to maintain my composure throughout the luncheon. It should have been a joyous occasion as many dignitaries were bestowing well wishes upon me. I was meeting former Presidents and every major living political figure of my lifetime. These seemingly untouchable leaders were congratulating me. But I could only wonder if my new friend President Worth had betrayed me. And even if he hadn't, what would his reaction be when he learned that his own father was corrupt. He said it himself, his father was his hero. He was the man that Daniel had patterned his life after. I always wondered how good men could become corrupt when elected to office. It was becoming clear that it would be very easy, maybe even essential.

In an ironic twist of fate, I was seated at the same table as George Worth and his wife, Emily. For the first thirty minutes the table had a line of well wishers that stopped by to congratulate the Senator on his son's success. As the lunch started being served, the line stopped and everyone found their seats.

"Did you ever see a day when your son would become President?" I asked the Senator.

The old man gleefully replied "One can only hope. Daniel is a good boy with a great vision for this country. I knew from a very young age that he had the qualities to lead this country but you just never know."

"It must be comforting to him to have a father with so much experience. I'm sure that he will lean on you quite a bit."

"I am more than happy to help him. But Daniel has always had his own way of looking at things. He is his own man."

God I hope so, I thought. I stared into the Senator's eyes when asking the next question.

"So what do you think of the New World Project, Senator? Your son has been the man that made it all possible."

"I think that it helped him get elected" he answered with a hint of skepticism.

"Do you believe in it?" I asked.

The Senator contemplated the question. "I believe that the people needed hope and this brings it to them."

"Can we pull it off?" I asked.

"We'll see about that."

I could see that the Senator was uncomfortable. He wanted to get off of the topic which only made me want to push it more but I decided to fall back a bit.

"Tell me about your mantra Sir. It seems like a pretty good saying to live by."

"It's just something that I have always believed in. I had a group of very dear friends that I served with years ago and that was our motto."

"The word sacrifice is the key for me. You have to ask yourself every day what true sacrifice means."

The old man did not care to be sitting beside a young kid, especially a kid that probed as much as I did. He started a conversation with the other people at the table but I had what I needed.

After an hour of presentations to the President and a five course meal, the luncheon started to wind down. I followed George Worth to the restroom and luckily it was empty as I made my way to the urinal next to him. I was tired of running, tired of guessing and tired of the entire establishment in which I had become a member. As I unzipped my pants, I decided that I was just going to go for it.

"So when do you plan to kill me?" I asked matter of factly.

"Excuse me" the old Senator replied.

"You've killed everyone in Supero, so when are you planning on killing me?"

The old man's face did not change. He stared directly at the wall in front of him as he continued doing his business.

"What makes you think that I would want to kill you kid? Where is this coming from?"

"You know that I saw the tapes and you are making everyone else with knowledge of Supero disappear, so I know that I am next."

"What in the hell are you talking about?" he asked in an unconvincing voice.

"You know exactly what I'm talking about you disgusting piece of old dried up dung. I'm tired of the stupid games. You are the Enforcer, I know that you are the Enforcer so don't try to hide it. I know your game and I know that you tried to have me killed." I zipped up my fly and faced the old Senator.

George Worth zipped up his pants and faced me. The rage in his eyes was menacing.

"You will not ruin this day for me and my family. You little snot nosed prick. You can not begin to understand what Supero has done for you and for this country. The reason that we are standing here today is because of that group. No one and I mean no one will ever stand in its way. I will kill you, that is a promise. You don't know the time and you don't know the place, but you will die a painful death."

"What about your son? Is Daniel in on this?" I asked the question that I had to know the answer to. In some crazy way, I needed the answer more than I needed to save my own life.

"My son has no affiliation with my beloved group. He is far too soft to ever be a part of something so powerful. He is an idealist with moral convictions that will be his downfall."

"So you tried to have him killed? You tried to kill your own son!"

The old man's anger hit its peak with that comment. He was willing and ready to kill me with his bare hands right there in the bathroom. His face was shaking with anger as his forehead turned a bright shade of crimson.

"I did not try to kill my son" he proclaimed while emphasizing every word.

"Someone did" I very calmly replied.

"And that someone is dead."

"So what are you going to do now George?"

"You will not address me as George. It is Senator Worth to you."

"So what are you going to do now George?" I replied while emphasizing the word George. "Are you going to run your little group behind Daniel's back?"

"Supero will reign forever. And your level of respect is disgusting. I would kill you right here if I could get away with it."

"You didn't answer my question, George. What are you going to do now? Your boy is in the White House. Are you going to run Supero without his knowledge?"

"My son will do as I tell him, he always has."

"Well, it's a one man group now isn't it George. You killed off everyone else."

"I did what I had to do. Without my group, our world would be a disaster. We have maintained world peace and have given this country a level of prosperity that has never been seen."

"But at what cost?" I replied. "You killed innocent children with a strain of the flu. You took away good jobs from the people that built this country with their bare hands. And you brought our enemies into your group. My Lord, you set up China to take our place as the next super power."

"I have done no such thing. You are ignorant and naïve. You believe in ideals that are not attainable. People need to be led, they want to be led. And the power in this country was shifting to a middle class that didn't know what to do with it. You will die young man and your asinine plan will die with you. I am in control and that will never change!"

"Your son will never stand for this."

"My son will never know."

"How do you sleep at night? You start and end wars, release deadly viruses, start recessions that put people on the streets and you somehow justify it as being for the greater good. You're a sick, sick man."

"You don't need to understand why we do what we do. Someone of your minuscule intellect would not be able to ever comprehend how we rule. And that is exactly why the group will always remain invisible. You are weak and unable to grasp the true meaning of order. You allow emotion to get into the way of reality. And your stupid, stupid little project has cost good men their lives. If you didn't come around, Supero would be intact. It is because of you that the group has been compromised."

"Thank God that I came around you sick old bastard. You were going to bomb a basketball game. Who does that?"

The creaking of an opening stall door startled us both. We thought that we were alone but we were definitely wrong. Daniel Worth appeared and slowly approached his father. He stared him straight in the eyes with the love and confusion that only a son could give after hearing something so horrific.

"Dad, tell me that this isn't true. Please dad, tell me that you didn't just say what you said."

Daniel Worth had been in the stall and heard the entire conversation. I was dumbfounded and very uncomfortable but was also now sure that my friend was not involved with Supero. George Worth looked defeated and disappointed.

"Son, you need to understand that everything that I have done is in the best interest of this country. I don't expect you to condone Supero's actions, but you know me and you know that I would never do anything unless it was in the best interest of our country." He stepped toward his son and put one arm on each of his son's shoulders, staring him directly in the face.

"Daniel, I have gotten you this far because you have trusted me. Now I need you to continue to trust me. On the surface, the things that we have done seem bad and I understand that. But you must realize that nothing was ever done without purpose. People want to be led and they want you to lead them. But we must control the world through wealth disparity. If we control them, then we can affect the outcome. If we lose control, then we can affect nothing."

"So it's true then isn't it?" the President asked.

"You're group started the war in Iraq, released flu viruses that had people killed and you were planning another attack on American soil. I want you to look me in the eyes and tell me it's true."

"Son, fear is a powerful tool. And yes we sacrificed a few for the benefit of many. I do not expect you to understand but you need to trust me. I know that you trust me. We can take this country to unprecedented heights. And your friend there can go along for the ride. But you must know that the things that I have done were for the love that I have for this country and its people."

The new President was crushed. It was the biggest day in his life and he was dealt a death blow. Only hours after delivering a speech that motivated millions, everything that he knew and loved had changed. The principles that he had patterned his life after were destroyed.

He stared into his father's eyes as I watched, uncertain as to how he would respond.

"You are dead to me."

Daniel Worth knew that he would have to make unfathomable choices during his presidency but he was not prepared for the first of many bombshells that he would encounter. Not only was he going to have to turn on his father and hero, but he was also going to have to deliver horrible news to his mother, his wife and the grandchildren that idolized their grandpa.

On the very first day that he became the most powerful man in the world, President Worth and his family would endure an embarrassment that would never escape his legacy. The entire framework of everything that he believed in was shattered on the day that was to be his crowning achievement. It would take time to realize that his beliefs were real even though his mentor taught under false pretenses.

CHAPTER 38

Five Years Later

Location – Washington DC

I was nervous when I knocked on her door. I had wanted to date Kristin for over two years. Today is the go live date on the New World Project and since we will no longer be working together, we decided to try a date to see where things might go.

"Hello Wes" she said as she opened her door. She was stunning. Her shoulder length blond hair was curled just a bit. Her flawless face did not need much make-up but the dark eyeliner that she used to accentuate her mesmerizing blue eyes was the perfect touch. The gloss on her full lips looked very inviting and she wore a mini dress that was cut just low enough in the front to barely expose her large chest. The dress accentuated her round but firm backside so needless to say she looked amazing.

"Are you just going to stand there or are you going to come in?" she asked.

"I'm sorry, you just look amazing. You always look amazing, but wow."

She smiled from embarrassment then replied "You look pretty amazing yourself." She then stood on her toes in order to reach my face and gave me a soft wet kiss on the lips.

"This night is going to be a blast" I said.

"Speaking of tonight, we are we going?" she asked.

"Well, this afternoon we are going to travel to Chicago and have lunch at the Italian Village. From there we are going to tour the Monet exhibit at the Art Institute of Chicago. And then I thought that tonight, we would travel to New York to see a concert at the New York Philharmonic and then enjoy dinner in New York before coming home tonight."

"This new world is going to be fun" Kristin replied. "I am so excited."

"I'm excited to be spending it with you" I replied.

This would be the first trip that I took in my new tram, a Ford X3000. Ford gave me the tram and I was more than happy to accept. The price tag on it was ten thousand dollars. I opened the door for my date and her eyes popped out of her head. We shut the door, entered our first destination into the computer and then snuggled together on the couch of my tram. I opened the refrigerator and poured two glasses of champagne to celebrate the culmination of our hard work. The New World Project had become a reality and we were about to truly experience it for the first time. As the world flew by at five hundred miles per hour I looked at my date and made a toast.

"To dreams" I said

"And to new beginnings" she replied.

And then we enjoyed the greatest night of our lives.

16720443R00150

Made in the USA
Charleston, SC
07 January 2013